UNDER THE MANGO TREES

THE CORAL SERIES
BOOK 1

UNDER THE MANGO TREES

A NOVEL

JENNIFER ODOM

WordCrafts Press

Dedicated to a true Cuban hero, Oscar Rafael Leyte Vidal
10/13/1936–2/16/2018

I've learned one thing for sure. A friend—or an enemy—is not always who we think they are. And it only took me twenty years to figure it out.

Chapter 1

Rosella.

Everyone called her that.

And so did I—up until the day she wrapped an arm around me and led me away from the principal's office. "Start calling me Grandma from now on," she whispered in my ear, "you hear me? I'll be your Grandma Rosella."

I was twelve when we first met, and she found me huddled in the sand between the roots of a mango tree.

I'd eventually wonder why my uncombed hair and bare feet didn't put her off, or my ragged tee shirt and thin cotton shorts. But I was thankful they hadn't.

I'd recently told myself that kids my age were too big to cry anymore over stuff like what had just happened in Mama's trailer. So with eyes burning I pinched off a string of snot and raked my tears across a sleeve. *Nope, no more crying for me.*

Even so, things seemed to be piling up really bad right about then.

Stars twinkled overhead as I wondered for the millionth time why my mama couldn't be like all the other moms at school. Even for one day.

It had to be after midnight. Mama's shift had ended. She had just gotten back to our trailer from her new waitressing job at a truck stop.

I'd been curled up in the front room on my pallet and had fallen into a deep sleep. The next thing I knew Mama was slapping at my legs, waking me up, and yanking me to my feet. I wobbled, bleary-eyed, against the flimsy wood paneling.

She, barely able to stand by herself, leaned into my face, her features dim in the low light and her eyes stark black. Slurred whiskey words puffed against my eyes. "Ma' boyfriend 'n' I have ta talk. Go ou'side. I'll call you back in later."

Not again.

Dull from sleep, I blinked and cut my eyes toward the front door as I tried to wrap my head around the situation.

"Go, Coral. Now. Go ou'side."

I listed in the direction of the door, grabbed its frame, and extended a bare foot toward the concrete blocks. Backtalk wouldn't have made a difference.

Her guy-of-the-night, a bulky silhouette, stood outside, thick arms crossed over his biker's vest. He lowered them as I stepped down.

"Well, well, well, Baby," he murmured.

I doubt if Mama heard or even noticed him pat my behind on the way down.

Or maybe she did.

I slapped his hand away and dodged. *Idiot.*

I'd never seen this person before, and I was glad to leave. Three's a crowd in that broken-down travel trailer.

Thank goodness she sent me out. I didn't trust her men. And if this one was like most of the others, I'd probably never see him again.

What scared me most were the ones who returned.

Mama always lied about calling me back inside after these *talks.* She always forgot. If I intended on returning to my pallet, I'd have to keep an eye open for her guy to drive away.

Tonight, considering her heavy alcohol, she'd likely be passed out cold, and I'd have to wake her up to go to work tomorrow.

Twenty feet away, between our trailer and the neighbors' trailer, I spotted the only furniture-like thing around, a big mango tree, and plopped down in the sand between its roots. I shifted and squirmed, and eventually, finding no comfort at all, just propped against its rough bark. It was hard to keep my eyes from burning, but the tears crept up anyway.

But they had nothing to do with my lack of comfort and everything to do with truth.

And the truth was, Mama, the only important person in my entire life, didn't care a hoot about me, or whether the mosquitoes, the iguanas, or even the alligators ate me up.

More than anything, I wished I could lock our front door and keep Mama's men out. But I had no idea how to fix the front door knob.

And it wasn't like I could run away. There was nobody else, no father, cousins, uncles, aunts, or even grandmas to escape to.

Just me and Mama.

And I only held onto her by a thread.

Once in a while she'd say she loved me, but every few days, no matter how hard I loved her back, she'd remind me how I tied her down, like I was some stray dog who cost too much to feed.

We ate a lot of peanut butter, eggs, and bread. And I tried not to eat too much. But I always got hungry again.

I wiped a palm across my face and hugged my knees and wished above everything else that I'd thought to drag a pillow out with me.

There was little chance of sleeping against the tree. Thank goodness, though, for the warm summer nights of South Florida.

Despite that, a chill ran over me, and goosebumps covered my arms. I shivered and tried to rub them away.

Crickets chirped loud, and a breeze rustled the leaves. Streetlights threw their shifting shadows over the dead windows of our trailer, the ugliest worst place of the whole park.

I twisted sideways to find a little comfort for my behind, but found none. The sand, gritty and white, formed a connection between our house and the neighbors on the right. Nobody lived on our left. Their yard seemed like a pretty photo with its large pale flowers, colorless now in the moonlight, and the white seashell path up to their front gate. So beautiful. I turned away again.

I didn't feel beautiful, not with my ugly bed-head and a cry-baby face, and I determined once again to "dry it up" like Mama always said, because "crying only made things worse." After all, she reminded me, I was nearly a teenager now.

Thankful for the darkness, I took a deep breath and wiped my burning eyes on the other sleeve.

The line of trees between our two places hid me well enough from the street, and I could have stayed there unnoticed for a long, long time. Except for the neighbors' dog.

Undetected by the girl, and nestled among the branches of the mango tree, Parapet the angel placed his fingers to his lips and whistled for the dog, a sound only the dog could hear.

Behind me the muffled bark of a little dog started up inside the neighbors' travel trailer.

Uh oh.

I turned and squinted as strings of lights came on, showing off the neighbors' scalloped awnings and wooden deck. Mango leaves now sparkled around me. The neighbors' whole yard, with its feathery palms and hibiscus border, now glowed in full color like a Christmas wonderland in mid-May.

Their front door squeaked open, and I backed into the shadows, holding my breath, and hoping they kept their dog inside.

Since we'd moved in a few weeks ago, we'd kept to ourselves. I'd never even met the neighbors. I had no idea what they were like, or if their dog was nice or mean.

The sound of tiny paws raced through the yard, and suddenly a huffing breathless dog, not much bigger than a shaggy rat, was bouncing all around my shoulders, licking my cheeks, and covering me with sand.

Flashlight beams danced left and right and illuminated the long-stemmed mango fruits that dangled like ornaments above me. I tensed as footsteps approached. The rays found my face and paused.

All I could think was, *Please don't call the police.*

From behind the light came the frail broken voice of an old lady. "Would you look at that? I thought I heard someone out here."

My one arm shielded my eyes, and I squinted once again, trying to see who was there. I used the other hand to wipe my face one more time and hide the tears.

"There, there. What's wrong, honey? What's your name?"

As many times as I'd been booted out of our trailer, I'd never been discovered outside like this before. I stood, sniffing and brushing off my backside. What could I say to someone who was nice enough to call me honey and ask what was wrong? "It's Coral. Coral Smith."

She reached her hand out for mine. There was nothing to do but let her take it. Her fingers were smooth and warm like butter that had sat in a dish all day. "Are you my new neighbor?"

I nodded as she held onto my hand and led me to her front deck.

"Well, my name's Rosella Flores, and this little doggie is Yap Yap." She paused and studied me up and down. "And I'm just wondering if you like cookies."

More nods and cheek-wiping and a running of my fingers through my messy hair.

She leaned close for me to catch her clean soap smell and smiled. "Oh, what a pretty little thing you are."

Me?

She indicated a chair up on the platform. "Why don't you sit out here while I go inside and tell Eduardo everything's okay. I'll be right back with those cookies and an Afghan too, if you want it."

She waited for my nod.

Rosella—with white braids like a halo on top of her head, she was only a little taller than me, and round where I was skinny. She lifted her pink nightgown above her slippers and traipsed up the steps.

Halfway inside she turned to look back. "We'll sit out here, and you can tell me all about it, what's going on, and why you're sitting out here all alone crying in the middle of the night."

Rosella returned with a plate of cookies and napkins and set them on the table between us. The big soft cookies reminded me of the peanut butter ones in the school cafeteria. She went inside again and returned with a little blanket over her arm—I guessed that was the afghan—and two glasses of milk.

"Here now." She wrapped the afghan around me and nudged the cookies close. "Help yourself to as many as you can eat." Then she seated herself with a cookie in her own hand. "I've noticed I always get hungry around midnight, too."

How could I not love this sweet little lady?

Dear Rosella.

I imagine she was the first person in the whole world to take an interest in me.

Before I knew it, she had coaxed all my sorrows out of me. I'm sure she already knew about everything at our place, though, with all Mama's screaming and bad words. The names she called me. We didn't have air conditioning, and the windows that weren't already broken stayed wide open.

"I know you love your mother very much, Coral. She's your mama, after all."

I had nothing to say to that. All I could do was picture Mama in her waitress dress and apron.

"Why don't you let me pray and break the power of all those bad words off you?"

I tipped my head, not sure what she was talking about.

"They're *on* me?"

"Let me show you something." She stepped inside and turned off the string of lights. My eyes had to get used to the dark all over again.

She took me by the hand. "Come. Walk to the gate with me."

Seashells crunched underfoot as she led me down the path and pointed up past the palm fronds to the sky. "See those stars? They're millions of miles away, and if you reached that farthest star there would still be more beyond it. The universe goes on and on."

We gazed at the twinkling pinpricks for the longest time.

"God is here with us. But He goes way past all that too. He made every bit of it. He's sooo big."

But what did that have to do with bad words?

"Bad words, good words, you can't see them, but they go on and on, traveling through space with no end. All of them."

I frowned. It sounded hopeless.

"Don't worry. We can fix it. We'll pray in Jesus's name and break the bad ones and put a stop to them if you like."

And that night was the first time I ever saw or heard of anointing oil.

Crickets cricked their summer song, and the breeze tickled my face as we stared up into the heavens. "Look," I said. A shooting star crossed behind a silent plane. Its red and green light blinked a path from one side of the mango branches to the other. I tried to imagine how far away the stars beyond it reached into that glittery space.

Eventually Rosella took my hand. "Let's go back and turn the lights on. There's something in my purse I want to get."

I took my chair again, and by the time she stepped back out of her trailer I'd eaten half of another cookie. "These are the best cookies in the world."

"Anytime you want to learn to make them, Coral, I'd love to teach you."

Me make cookies? I chewed, gazing at her as she took her seat. I couldn't imagine creating something like a cookie. My own mama couldn't cook.

By then I'd almost forgotten about breaking the bad words.

She opened her palm to show me a tube-thing of oil with a lid. A *vial*, I'd soon learn. "Here it is—anointing oil. You want the bad words broken off you?"

I nodded hard.

She unscrewed the lid, dampened her fingertip, and then leaned forward and drew a little cross on my forehead. "I anoint you in the name of the Father, Son, and Holy Spirit. And I break those bad words and curses off of you in the name of Jesus."

I closed my eyes and waited.

"That's all there is," she said, and I opened them again.

"I don't feel anything."

"Did you feel the bad words?"

I shrugged. "Inside, I guess."

She smiled and put the lid back on. "You don't have to feel it."

I nodded.

"This oil marks you as Jesus's own little girl."

I closed my eyes and let that idea settle over me. I didn't quite understand it, but if she liked Jesus—well, I did too.

Behind me I heard the sound of our trailer's front door opening. I didn't turn around. Mama's guy must be leaving. After a minute the motorcycle revved up, and even though the engine made a fairly quiet *burp-burp-burrrrrrr*, it grew louder and blasted a hole through the night.

We listened as it faded into the distance.

I stood. "I guess it's time to go back to the trailer." When she stood too, I hugged her around her small nightgown-covered shoulders. I couldn't help myself. "Thank you, Rosella, for everything."

"Take some cookies with you. Take some for your mother. Remember what I told you, too. I meant it."

She didn't need to persuade me. "May I..."

"Yes, come back anytime, honey. Anytime you like. Day or night. Even the middle of the night like tonight. Make sure to get your mama's permission, though."

And after that, it wasn't long until I met Eduardo, the love of Rosella's life.

Chapter 2

From that point on you couldn't tear me away from Rosella's.

Oh, I wanted to head back over to her house the very next morning. But Mama slept in. Mama didn't much care how I spent my time, one way or another, as long as I stayed home while she worked. That was rule number one. Of course, that meant I read a lot. A whole, whole lot.

The other rule was to never ever wake her from sleep except to tell her it was time to go to work.

So I stayed home that morning with my mind's eye still picturing Rosella in her long pink nightgown.

The second morning, though, as soon as I could, I knocked on my newly-discovered neighbor's door.

And I was totally unprepared.

There, at the top of the steps, under a summer straw hat with a huge pink flower and wide ribbon, was a transformed Rosella in perfect makeup. Rosella smiled down at me, like a tiny movie star in hot pink lipstick. I stared open-mouthed at the prettiest little old lady I had ever seen. She could have been heading out to a party.

Thinking back, that day must have been a Saturday because I would soon learn that Rosella had rules too. She wore a specific color for each day of the week. And Saturday was pink day.

The wild print of her Hawaiian dress reflected the day's rosy color.

Speechless, I stared.

"Coral! Good morning. Did you get permission from your mother?"

I nodded, bug-eyed.

The cookies I'd brought home had seriously impressed Mama's

sweet tooth. Having a baker next door boosted all my chances of hanging out with Rosella again.

Rosella would require permission for every visit, but I soon discovered Mama enjoyed giving it. Though sometimes because of her late hours, I had to write little notes for her to sign like I had to do for school.

"We're taking a walk around the square, and I don't want your mama upset with me."

I raised my right hand. "I promise. I did get permission."

"Nope. Nope. No promising. Let your yes be yes and your no be no. Anything more than that comes of evil, don't you know?"

I didn't know, and I found out later that Rosella got that straight from her Bible.

"In fact," she added, "don't trust anybody who says *I promise.*"

"Yes, then."

Rosella climbed down the metal steps, slid them out and over to the side, and away from the lift. I hadn't noticed its steel base flattened against the deck the other night, probably because of the wrought iron railings mounted all the way around it. At first glance it seemed like part of the front deck.

Rosella pushed a button near the bottom of the doorframe and we rode up, railings and all, to the front door.

"Neat," I said when it stopped, "an elevator."

"It is, I guess. A young man invented it for me." She stepped inside and wrangled a folded wheelchair out the door.

I squeezed against the railing to stay out of the way.

"A very nice boy," she said, "and he's about your age—he's the one who invented, or thought it up. Can you imagine that? Your same age?" She opened the seat and locked the wheelchair's wheels. "He said if a van could have a lift—well, my travel trailer could have one too. The only tricky part is getting the chair in and out this door. But we manage."

A tall man with a walker appeared at the door.

"Coral, meet my husband, Eduardo." She reached up and patted his cheek. It was smooth, like he'd just shaved. "The love of my life."

Eduardo gave me a big smile and a wink as he eased through

the doorway with his walker. His left leg dragged. Even for an older man he was handsome—with those dark eyes, dark olive skin, and thick white hair. He lowered himself in the wheelchair, then folded and propped the walker against the railing. Both his arms worked fine.

I'd imagined that Eduardo would be a small man, not tall. In his youth he must have been crazy handsome, with those even white teeth and face-creasing smile. He smelled fresh too, like orange peel and crushed leaves, not like the sweaty men who visited our place.

The love of her life. I certainly understood.

She explained about his stroke. "Eduardo has no use of his left leg, and he's lost his speech. But I'll assure you he has *not* lost his mind."

Come to think of it, his face did droop a little on the left.

After he was seated, Rosella kissed the top of Eduardo's head and locked the door. She reached inside the doorframe, pushed a button at waist level, and the ramp came right on down to the concrete.

"I don't care for the utilitarian appearance of ramps," Rosella said at the bottom, unlocking the wheels. She pushed the wheelchair off the ramp and the deck, then along the path of hard-packed sand and seashells. It surprised me that the wheelchair could roll over a surface like that, but it did.

The pink wedge heels on Rosella's feet didn't slow her down either.

On the way to the gate, we passed by a round concrete table and matching curved benches. Their surfaces gleamed with tiles—artsy ceramic ones done up in pictures of pink flamingos and bright red flowers.

I ran my fingers over its smooth top. "A real *mosaic,*" I said. "We learned about these at school."

I glanced up at the tall flower bushes between our yards. Massive clumps of bamboo divided our back yards. No wonder I hadn't seen this table before. One good thing, though, the bushes also blocked her view of our trailer. No one should have to look at that ugly thing.

"Eduardo's game table," Rosella said. "You'll learn more about that when we get back."

She brought me close and showed me how to press the spring latch on the wire gate. The metal curlicue on top reached my chest.

Green ivy grew through the antique arches of the gate's twisted wires. Along this ancient fence and at both ends of her yard grew masses of fuchsia bougainvillea that climbed high into the palm trees. Closer to the gate grew a hedge of red hibiscus and yellow flowers that Rosella later taught me were called allamandas. These covered most of the actual fence. But I could still tell it was under there.

She pushed the wheelchair through the gate. "Make sure to snap the gate shut so Eduardo's friends know he's out. "His buddies are pretty old, and I don't want them walking all this way for nothing."

We strolled up the street and around the corner to downtown, then circled the square a few times before stopping for a few minutes at the office of Mr. Peter Cordero, Attorney. After Rosella introduced me, she and Mr. Cordero chatted a bit. He seemed eager to see Eduardo and leaned down to hug him. Eduardo seemed happy to see the attorney as well.

Though Eduardo could only nod or use a little sign language to answer, Peter asked about his welfare and how his other relatives were doing.

"Like family, these two," Rosella said. "They go way back, to when Peter's father was alive. I'll tell you about it sometime." I soon learned that stopping by Mr. Cordero's place was a daily custom on their walks.

Rosella said we had to get back home, so we all shook hands, hugged and kissed over both shoulders, a new custom to me, and one that I really liked, and bid each other a good morning.

On the way home, Rosella and Eduardo waved at and visited with several more acquaintances, then we made a pit-stop at the city restrooms.

"It's easier for Eduardo to get in here," Rosella explained as he wheeled himself into the spacious men's room.

"I really liked Mr. Cordero," I told her.

"Like the man said, you can call him Peter. He's your friend now, too. Eduardo has lots of friends, nice folks, and before you know it, they'll all be your friends too."

Soon after our walk I found out what she meant. It didn't take long to get adopted into the Grandpas and Elderly Uncles Club.

Chapter 3

It was around 10 am when we returned from our walk. We entered the gate and left it hanging open this time, the signal for Eduardo's friends to come on down. From any front yard along the street, a person could look straight down the shady sidewalk and see that vine-covered gate hanging open over the sidewalk.

Rosella parked Eduardo at the mosaic table where he had a good view left and right across the street.

Eduardo brought something out of his shirt pocket that looked like a pack of cigarettes. He dumped it in his hand, and out slid a deck of cards which he began shuffling.

Rosella steered me toward the house. "Come inside, Coral, and let's bring out the goodies."

Goodies?

"And I'll teach you how to make Cuban coffee."

"Mama drinks instant."

"Does she? I bet she'd like this. It's mighty sweet." We stepped back under the scalloped deck covering whose bright stripes of yellow and white I hadn't even noticed the other night. Rosella dragged the metal steps back in place so we could get inside. "Most weekdays Eduardo's friends spend time with him. That mosaic table you were admiring is their gathering place."

"A club?"

She nodded.

I followed Rosella into her trailer and paused to gaze around the cozy room with its pristine yellow and white polka dot theme. The crisp colors of her outdoor awnings had followed us inside like a blast of sunshine. She hardly needed to turn on the lights.

"Everything's so tidy and clean."

"Well, as they say, a place for everything and everything in its place."

Rosella's trailer, compared to our cramped space next door with its dark walls and bundles of belongings piled here and there, was a total contrast.

Here I found perfect order. My mouth hung open as I rotated, taking it all in.

Over in the kitchen to our left Rosella hooked up a coffee pot. She pointed to a tray on top of the small refrigerator. "Bring that down, and I'll let you arrange the cookies."

I reached for them. *More* cookies? She must have an unending supply of those things.

I set them on the table and lifted the ruffled front curtain to peek into the front yard. Eduardo's elderly friends had filtered in, five of them, all happy-looking, and took seats at his table. Two had cigars.

I turned and watched Rosella fill the coffee pot, and then she helped me line up the cookies. Behind her, taped to her refrigerator door, was a list of names and a collection of what must have been Rosella's family photos. I recognized two pictures of Eduardo, a small one taken when he was about my age, and another more recent one taken during his older years. And there were other photos of men, maybe the ones outside. A small oily spot topped each item. I tapped the picture of a round-faced man whose light-colored hair clearly resembled Rosella's and turned.

"My son," she said, before I could speak. "And he's got one son, my only grandson. They're in Vegas."

"Las Vegas?"

Her gaze dropped to the items on the table. She said no more.

Her son. I nodded. Had he died or something? *And what about the grandson?*

I moved my finger to the list on a yellow paper. "What's this list of names? Hey, there's my name on the bottom."

That brought a smile. "My friends. It's a prayer list."

She nodded toward the photos. "They're all on it."

I peered through the curtains again at Eduardo's visitors while the coffee machine gurgled and hissed. "If he can't talk, how does he have so many friends?"

"Oh, my," she said, arranging coffee cups on a second tray and filling them. "He's a hero. Those men out there? He saved their lives, including Peter Cordero's father. And then he went back and brought others to safety, too."

She gathered her tray, and I gathered mine.

I was friends with a real live hero?

What had Eduardo done?

We brought the cookies and coffee outside. There were just enough cups for the men.

"Seis? Six cups only? Rosella," one of them said. His deep voice resounded in a beautiful Spanish accent. "How could you? Don't deprive this little child of your wonderful Cuban coffee."

The coffee's delicious aroma had driven me crazy ever since Rosella started the pot. "Mama won't care," I assured her.

She eyed me, but tilted her head in doubt.

"Really," I said. "I drink Mama's instant coffee all the time at home."

The mention of instant coffee brought a negative murmur from the men. Apparently, it was a bad thing around here.

Rosella gave in with a laugh. "Oh, all right. If you all insist." Then she went back inside for a cup for me, too.

She returned with an ice-chip melting in my coffee. I took a sip and closed my eyes. "Like heaven," I said. The mens' appreciative comments warmed the air. Rosella's brew was the most fabulous drink I'd ever tasted, and I was quick to say so. On that day I was spoiled. Spoiled forever.

Maybe that's why the Grandpa and Elderly Uncles Club adopted me right away. I loved their coffee.

I hoped they weren't just being kind.

Though Eduardo was similar in age, I imagined him as the grandpa in the group and secretly as my own. I had no other. The uncles were called tío José, tío Octavio, tío Edmundo, tío Fernán, and tío Ricardo. Tío means *uncle*.

Tío Segundo, Peter Cordero's father, had already passed away. Peter, a lawyer, was younger than all of these men, of course, and though he was part of their club he had a law office to run and didn't have time to play cards every day.

The rest of the men, a couple of them widowers, lived in the nearby lots of our place, the Palm Breeze Trailer Court and Retirement Village. I'm not sure how Mama at her young age got permission to move in, but our old trailer was such an ugly duckling, or rather baby buzzard, of the neighborhood that maybe nobody else would have it. I was glad though, and I hoped we stayed a good long while.

The men scooted together and made a spot for me at the end of one bench. When they insisted I learn their game, *cubiletes,* a game played with dice, Rosella laughed and disappeared back inside with her empty trays.

While we played, I suggested card games of my own, like *Uno* and *Old Maid.* But they said I had to learn theirs first and become very good at everything, a different Cuban game for each day, including checkers, chess, and dominoes, before they'd play my games.

That first day we played *cubiletes* though. Between rolls of the dice they taught me Spanish words like *gracias* for thank you, *por favor* which means please, and *tio* that means uncle, then cheered when I got them right. There were plenty of times I just had to guess what a word meant or think of a similar-sounding word in English. It was like a game for all of us.

Then tio Ricardo reached under his seat and set a box of cigars on the table. Two who didn't already have a cigar reached inside, but Eduardo, with Yap Yap perched on his lap, did not. They shared a little device from the box to cut the tips off, and used lighters from their pockets to twirl and light the ends of the cigars.

A fragrant cloud soon hovered over our table.

Tio Ricardo took a cigar. He eyed me, laughed, and pulled his *tabaco* away as if I would take it.

"Coral, *mija,* sorry. We have to draw a line at this one. We can let you share our *cafe,* but not our *tabaco.*"

I smiled, and though I really liked it I swatted the strong smoky air. "Ha. Anyway, I don't want your old cigars."

"Here," he said, sliding off the cigar's round label. It looked like a ring. "The *anillo* for you. Our new friend."

Everyone else donated their own anillo. I jammed them on, a ring for every finger and held up my hand. I was a queen. In the meantime, Rosella returned and filled the cups again. Mine was empty and instead of refilling it, Rosella brought me a glass of water.

"Thank you for the rings," I said to the men, fluttering my hand. I hovered it over tio Ricardo's freshly filled coffee cup. "But be nice, or I'll have to take your coffee!"

They howled with laughter and sent up another cloud of smoke.

My hair would smell of cigars for days, but I never had so many friends in my life, and I never had so much fun, either.

Chapter 4

Not long after I got to know all the uncles Rosella and I were taking another early morning stroll around the square with Eduardo. He'd brought along the dog this time, fit snugly beside him in the seat.

I'd been looking for this chance to grill Rosella about Eduardo's hero story. "How did he do it? How did he save them?"

She gave me a sideways glance. "Have you heard of Cuba?"

"Sure. Cuban coffee, remember?" But I had no idea where Cuba was.

She pointed south. "Head that way, to the sunny sands of Key West, and then sail ninety more miles over crystal blue waters."

Rosella wagged a finger. "Don't let that beauty deceive you, though." She slowed Eduardo's chair and put on a serious face, sweeping her hand across a large imaginary expanse of sea. "One minute it will sparkle in the sun and reflect the most beautiful blue sky.

"But then," she leaned close, "a dark storm blows in. The deep turns black as night. And waves big enough to sink a ship rise higher and higher, tossing grown men into the sea where they paddle for their lives and beg for mercy that the sharks won't eat them alive."

A chill crawled up my spine.

Eduardo reached behind his shoulder and gripped Rosella's hand. He must have sensed what I did. She returned the squeeze, an unspoken message of some kind.

"It's still so real to us," she said, "Eduardo lived through it, and told me all the stories."

I clung to her elbow as we moved on. I didn't want to miss a word.

"But there on the other side lies a green tropical land rich with gardens and sandy beaches. Orange and banana trees, mangoes, coconut palms, and beautiful music decorate the land. Cuba. Loveliness filled the air. That was Eduardo's home *before*."

"Like this? Ft. Myers?" I asked. How much more beauty could be there than our royal palms and flowers everywhere?

She held up one finger. "But then, along came a wicked leader. He hurt people, locked them in jails, and killed so many others. And if anyone disagreed with his evil schemes, he confiscated their businesses, their homes, and even their children."

Rosella strolled on, and by the look on her face, was busy imagining all the hurt of those bad things.

"Castro." She spat the name. "That's who. A living demon."

I stared at her, waiting for more about him. But nothing came.

"Eduardo's family, very wealthy, didn't agree with this devil. And they spoke up. So Castro snatched away everything—their licenses to practice medicine and law, their bank accounts, their beautiful homes. He sent them off to live in shacks and work in the cane fields."

I couldn't take my eyes off her face. "Were you there too?" I wanted to know. It seemed so vivid to her.

"No, but as I said, Eduardo has described it—many times."

I waited.

"It was only a matter of time before Eduardo and his boyhood friends would be forced into the evil one's army," she continued. "'Will we join? Never!' they declared.

"But Castro had eyes and ears everywhere. 'We have to sneak away,' Eduardo whispered to his friends."

I gazed at the back of Eduardo's head and imagined him slipping through the night with his friends, dodging through the shadows between the trees.

She turned to me. "But Cuba is an island. How would they get off?"

"By boat?"

"Ah, every boat that a refugee could possibly take had already been seized. Times were desperate. The boys had to improvise."

"A plane?"

She shook her head.

I was all ears.

"Castro forbade young men to fly. They might escape. He needed them as soldiers. Anyway, Castro took all their money. How could they hope to pay for a plane trip?"

I nodded, wondering how it could happen.

"Those men you played cards with? Those were the friends. All five, and one more who has since passed away."

Peter Cordero's father.

"'We might die trying, but we have to get to America,' my Eduardo told them. 'And not just for us.'"

Eduardo, in his wheelchair, pressed a hand across his heart. Yap Yap shifted and groaned as if he were listening too.

Rosella continued. "And what did Eduardo tell them? 'We must also find a way to get our families out.'"

I interrupted, realizing all this time I'd been biting my lip. "Did they swim through the sharks?"

She smiled and held up one finger for me to wait and kept on with the story. "'We'll trust in you,' they told Eduardo. 'Show us the way.'"

"'Don't worry, I've got a plan,' he said."

By now, my heart was in my throat. "What was it?"

Rosella shook her head. "Oh, it was an impossible predicament."

She parked the wheelchair in the shade by a stone fence, and we sat. I gazed at Eduardo, my hero. He held Rosella's eye with an expression I didn't understand.

"'Borrow tools,' he said. 'Unbolt the tires of a big truck. Gather eight large inner tubes.'"

Rosella stretched her arms wide. "'Big ones like this. We'll fill them with air, pump them tight, and lash them together with ropes, all we can find. Across the top, we'll weave a platform of long bamboo stalks.'"

"There's a bunch of that growing between our back yards," I said.

She nodded. "It's immensely strong, you know."

But the boys would weigh down the inner tubes. "Could the sharks bite through them?" I asked.

Eduardo closed his eyes with a pained look across his forehead.

"I bet you prayed a *lot*," I said.

He nodded and gave the dog a pat.

I couldn't imagine being so brave.

Rosella continued. "'Before we leave,' Eduardo told his friends, 'scribble out your good-byes to your families. Then tell them to read and then destroy the notes. Or Castro will find the notes and hurt you.'"

I shook my head as Rosella continued.

"On a dark, moonless night they carried what food and water they could, and set out for the shore. There, in the breeze, with the warm sea lapping and foaming along the sand, they gathered their paddles and untied the raft where they'd hidden it among the mangroves. For a moment they knelt and whispered a prayer for safety, and then set to work tugging and dragging the raft into the waves. Finally, they pushed off into the deep and drifted away, paddling north, north, north under a twinkling mat of stars."

I shuddered.

"Days and days passed. They'd rationed out their food and water. By now it was nearly gone. With cracked lips, dehydrated and blistered by the sun, they could hardly speak. Oh, how they wanted to reach their hands into the cool water, to bring it up and sprinkle it over their poor baked skin."

Eduardo squeezed Rosella's hand.

"But sharks surrounded their float. Dozens."

They must not have bit the tubes.

"Black clouds darkened the western sky. 'It's a bad storm brewing,' Eduardo told them."

I wrapped my arms around myself and squeezed.

"A rain would have been nice, would have cooled the boys' skin. But instead, the sea darkened. It swelled and heaved. A stiff wind blew. With one eye on the clouds the boys lay flat. They lashed themselves to the bamboo mat. The little vessel bobbed, rising higher and higher on each crest then plummeting like a rock into the troughs, bruising their battered bodies. And each time it did they prayed they wouldn't flip and land upside down among the sharks. They wove their arms through the bamboo, their feet through ropes, closed their eyes, and held tight, as wave after wave washed over them. Yet their ropes held.

"'Oh, God, let the storm turn away, let it go in a different direction,' they prayed. But onward it came, closer and closer. Wind whipped the spray from the waves and burned their eyes. Their teeth chattered. Within minutes they'd switched from being sunburned and baking to being thoroughly chilled.

"And right when they thought they would surely be lost—'Look! Land, ho! There to the north.'

"So tipping and lurching, with goose bumps all over their shivering bodies, they stretched out their arms and paddled, all the while hoping and praying the sharks would not notice. But then a powerful current twirled them around. It snatched them east and that hope-filled glimpse of the shore slid farther and farther into the distance. They'd hit the mighty Gulf Stream. Now they sped northeast, around the tip of Florida. Once again, they entered the blazing sunshine. They'd left the storm behind.

"Hot and baking once again, they passed skyscrapers and planes and boats too far away to notice them. Then finally close enough to shout, they passed two fishermen pulling in their nets. Exhausted and desperate, the boys waved their blistered arms, *'Help us. Help us! Please!'* And they swept on by. The men, hearing their cries, and more sympathetic than some others might be, took note of their predicament, and loading up their tackle, followed. They drew near the raft, threw out ropes, and lifted the sick, starving boys into the boat. The men plied food and water on them and all the first aid they could come up with.

"Never were refugees more grateful than those boys."

I stared at Eduardo. He could have died. But here he sat, healthy and well now except for the wheelchair. How brave they all were to face such dangers.

Rosella smiled. "Thank God. The President of the United States understood, and after some time in a hospital the boys were allowed to stay."

I grinned at Eduardo.

"It was a very long process, but now they are *real citizens.*"

Tears welled up in my eyes. "You escaped from Castro." I leaned across the wheelchair and pressed my cheek against his strong rugged one. "I'm so glad you made it. You're so brave." We patted each other's back.

"And those friends at the card table," Rosella said. "Each one is a hero. But they might not have left Cuba, might not have had the courage if Eduardo hadn't convinced them. A true leader he was. You're mingling with some fine men, Coral. Fine, brave men." Rosella leaned down and kissed his other cheek. "Especially this one."

I took a deep breath.

"And then, there's the second part of the story."

More? I raised my eyebrows and listened.

"Each one of the boys were men now. They worked and worked for a very long time, saving every penny for their families. They sent it all back home to help them escape. For a time, all Cubans except the soldiers could fly. Some flew to Spain, and then doubled back to the States. Eduardo and his friends made homes for their moms and dads and sisters and brothers to come to."

She squeezed Eduardo's hand. "Amazing heroes."

But very soon, Rosella would become a hero. My hero.

Chapter 5

Rosella hadn't intentionally kept her cabana a secret. I just hadn't seen her back yard or walked out her back door before. And then there was that thick wall of bamboo growing between our back yards.

I might have eventually discovered the cabana on my own, but in the middle of May Mama and I had only been in the neighborhood a few weeks, and I'd been occupied with the difficult and awkward accomplishment of trying to make up the end of the school year with new teachers. What made things worse was that Mama always moved whenever the rent came past due, and that meant a lot of new schools for me. It made things very hard for me and cost me a whole failed school year.

That morning I stood in Rosella's kitchen pouring water into her coffeemaker. We were preparing for the Heroes Club, my newest name for the Grandpas and Elderly Uncles Club.

"Cookies are running low," Rosella said. "Let's go out back and fetch some more."

In the back yard? Who kept cookies back there?

As I followed I imagined her back steps would be made of concrete blocks—like the ones at our own front door. Our back door had no steps at all, only a huge drop-off the led down to some weedy woods and a creek. That made it pretty much useless. Rosella probably had nice steps, and I was curious to see.

But when she opened the door, I was unprepared. There was no drop-off. My wildest dreams couldn't have thought up what Rosella had in her back yard.

I gasped as she led the way out along a bright pink boardwalk. Yap Yap shot out between us and trotted ahead. I couldn't help but give a little squeal and peek around Rosella's shoulder to see what was up there. The walk extended about twenty feet to a floor, with three walls and a roof, about four times as big as her trailer.

The wall facing her trailer was not there. It was open like a big porch. "My cabana," she said, waving her arm toward it.

The pink boardwalk stood a good ten feet above a sandy creek-bank, the one thing our back yards did have in common. We shared a shallow five-foot-wide stream which flowed into the Caloosahatchee River and out to the Gulf of Mexico. At school we'd learned all about it.

"It's a paradise!" I blurted. Below us grew an array of banana trees, areca palms, and bird of paradise plants. We were walking across the top of Rosella's back yard.

I took in every detail of this place—the pickets, the rails that bordered the walkway, and the open-fronted cabana.

Rosella sure knew about color.

Every eight feet or so along the walk stood grooved pink four-by-four posts topped with lavender glass balls—lights, probably. Matching gingerbread trimmed the roof line beyond, but the contrast of the cabana's yellow and orange ceiling surprised me.

"It's like a fairyland. Or a birthday cake."

Rosella gave me her biggest smile and passed through the sunlight into the cabana. It turned her into a flaming angel before my eyes in that yellow and orange dress.

"Surround yourself with beauty, my dear. The good Lord created color. We should enjoy it."

I was more than thankful for the excuse to see this. What could I say? I turned around and around, gawking at the surroundings. "And I didn't even know this was here."

In the back, a small room with a closed door filled the left corner. An open-air kitchen with a sink, stove, and refrigerator filled the center, and on the right was another closed off room of some type.

In the front half sat a table surrounded by rose and lavender chairs, and in the center a sitting area complete with table, pillowed chairs, and lamps. Where the boardwalk ended, there was lots of extra floor space.

Rosella had enough room for guests back here.

She grinned, apparently satisfied at my amazement. "My artsy abode."

What a place. I stared at her, wishing I could move in.

"What if it rains?" I asked. The front side was completely open.

"You're a practical one, aren't you?"

She pointed up behind the gingerbread scallops to a long stretch of clear, rolled-up plastic. "We untie those bows and bring the walls down. And we pray for no hurricanes."

I hadn't even thought of that.

"We've certainly had storms. In that case we pack all the furniture into those rooms and seek shelter elsewhere. Nobody should stay in a mobile home or travel trailer in a hurricane."

I nodded. We had to do the same thing when I was eight. But that was in some other town.

She strode over to a bright green and yellow door by the refrigerator and pulled it open. "My cooking closet." She nodded toward a large plastic container of cookies on its middle shelf. "I made more cookies last night."

"Out *here*?"

"It's a little roomier out here, don't you think?"

I nodded.

Boxes and cans filled the shelves in a space as large as Rosella's entire travel-trailer kitchen.

"Pull those cookies out and bring them inside. I know you want to see more, but we can explore this some other time."

I followed behind as she led the way back down the boardwalk. Even from behind, minus her sun hat with its big orange flower, which she'd left on the table in the trailer, Rosella glowed. To me she was so beautiful.

She was such an artist. There were no paintings here. But her clothes, her home, its details, the way she lived—the way she *was*—that was her art.

And in that moment, I knew. I wanted to be just like her.

Yap Yap followed us back inside Rosella's trailer and into the kitchen where we arranged the cookies and coffee cups on the trays. "You have a perfect life, Rosella—like a fairy tale."

"Oh, no, child." She laid her hand on my arm. Her words came out thoughtful and slow. "Nobody has a perfect life. Don't ever think that. Everybody, eventually, has a burden of some type." She gave me a serious but loving look. "You have sorrows. I have sorrows."

What could possibly ruin things for her?

I must have frowned or looked surprised.

"Yes, I have sorrows, too."

I had to think about that. "Like Eduardo and his wheelchair?"

"Oh, dear Coral. I still *have* Eduardo. That's not a sorrow. I have his love. Of course, the stroke was terrible."

Some people might think differently, like it was the end of the world. I tended to agree with her, though.

"Oh, worse than that. Grief." She waved a hand across the photos on the refrigerator door. "Each person carries their share."

I studied the pictures on the door. *What kind of grief?* Rosella seemed so content.

"But grief can give us purpose. There is always hope."

Hope?

She picked up a tray, and so did I. I studied her face, trying to figure what Rosella's grief could be.

Chapter 6

Most weeks now, it seemed that Mama worked all seven days. I hardly saw her at all.

So Rosella and I spent a lot of time together. After hanging out and playing all kinds of card games with the Heroes Club each morning, the three of us ate lunch together—Rosella, Eduardo, and me. While Eduardo took cat naps with Yap Yap curled at his side or rolled his chair out to the cabana to work on jewelry, Rosella and I played Scrabble indoors. Since I read all the time, I was very good at the game, but Rosella was hard to beat.

She also taught me gardening.

On one of our morning walks with Eduardo, she stopped in at a garden shop and bought zinnias, marigolds, and impatiens for the yard and a pair of pink garden gloves and spade for me. At the dollar store she bought me a small fingernail brush.

"For you," she said. "And always wear gloves in the yard," she added.

I opened the package and put them on, prancing around behind the wheelchair with my spade. I'd never worn a glove in my life. I laughed. "People will think I'm prissy."

"Nah, you're keeping the microorganisms and insects off your hands and out of your nails. I can show you a picture sometime of a fungal nail infection. It's pretty nasty looking."

"Eww, gross!" I waved the thought away with the spade and dropped my new things back into the bag. "It's okay. I don't have to see it to believe it."

I was never one to examine wounds, and wouldn't want to be a nurse or doctor.

That afternoon I learned how to read plant labels to learn what grew in the sun or shade. Who knew flowers had preferences?

We planted our flowers then sprinkled a little fertilizer among them. "Not too much water or fertilizer," she told me. "Or you'll kill them. Plants can burn up or drown."

My head was buzzing. There was so much to know.

Over the summer she taught me names of all her flowers and plants, and many others that grew up and down the street.

But my favorite lesson was making cuttings, especially of the jewel-colored impatiens flowers. It amazed me that I could grow a new plant from just a stem.

From then on, I never looked at over-grown plants the same. Instead, I imagined how many cuttings they would make. For *free*.

Up until then I never gave much thought to what might be around the right side of Rosella's trailer. But out there, near the padlocked door of a large metal shed, she showed me a small wooden table. "Every gardener needs a potting bench," she said.

On top sat twelve little green pots filled with fresh potting soil and a tiny cup of white powder. Rosella must have come out earlier and set it all up. A water hose with a sprayer was hooked up in the grass beside it.

"You and I have all the flowers we can use," she said. "So here's where we plant our new cuttings to share with our neighbors." We'd been pruning the flowers, and she held up a handful of impatiens trimmings. "We could throw all this away and not think a thing of it. But we could also find a way to be generous and spread some joy."

"Or put them in a vase."

She nodded. "That's always a nice option." She divided out part of her handful and set it on the table. "Here. These are for the vase. But can you think of someone who would like some flower plants?"

She laid her trimmings on the table and showed me how to trim the leaves and locate the nodes. "Dip the bottom node into the white powder and make sure it goes down in the soil. That's where the new roots grow."

I picked up the stem and studied the nodes where the leaves had been snapped off.

"Now you try it."

She handed me clippers, and I trimmed a dozen more stems, leaving the tops like she had done.

"Perfect."

I beamed.

After she poked a hole in the soil with a stick, she had me dip the nodes into the rooting powder and insert the stem into the soil.

"Snug the soil around the stem and then water it gently with the sprayer."

"That's it?"

She nodded. "After a few weeks it will take off and start putting on new leaves."

We cleaned, up and she showed me how to use the fingernail brush.

Rosella knew how to make even everyday experiences a lot of fun. If only school were this great.

How amazing that a clipped-off stem with broken-off leaves would grow into something big.

I couldn't get enough of Rosella's lessons.

Another day Rosella found a metal watering can. We punched holes in the bottom with a hammer and old nail.

"We'll hang this up over the birdbath and build a dripper," she said. "Birds adore this."

And they did. Throughout the summer all kinds of birds visited the birdbath, and we looked up their names.

"I should write them down," I said.

That afternoon Rosella bought me a special journal with a mockingbird picture on the front. "Put the dates, too," she said. "Some of the birds are seasonal."

The hummingbirds with their jewel-like bodies and fast-beating wings became my favorites.

At the library we checked out bird books. Rosella also introduced me to what she called the *classics*. "Let's start with Charles Dickens and Louisa Mae Alcott."

A lover of books already, I had no objections and was glad for the suggestions. Rosella kept me well-supplied with books, and we made as many trips to the library as I wanted.

But one trip turned into a disaster.

Chapter 7

On our library walks we always passed a pretty ice cream shop with a porch and pink-and-white awnings. Its large, shaded windows were painted with storybook ice cream cones, banana splits, and chocolate sundaes with whipped cream and cherries.

But I'd never thought about us buying an ice cream there. In all my life I could count on one hand the times I'd had ice cream.

This day as we approached, Rosella slowed and turned to me. "How about we go in today and have a treat?"

Who would turn that down?

Up on the porch sat two girls about my age and maybe a little older, in matching sundresses. They took up the middle of a long bench as they licked their multi-flavored cones and watched us walk up. Rosella said good morning, and I held the door while she marched on in pushing Eduardo's chair ahead of her. I smiled at the girls as I closed it behind us. They had already ignored Rosella's greeting and now dismissed my smile by staring back at me like I was something from outer-space. Their blank looks expressed that we were invading *their* ice cream shop, and our company was not welcome.

Something was off.

I scuttled inside. We took our time selecting our flavors, and Rosella paid. Out on the porch, the two girls had twisted around to watch us. They laughed, shared looks, and talked between themselves.

The inside of the shop was empty of furniture. "Where are all your tables and chairs today?" Rosella asked.

"Sorry," the ice cream man said. "It's just until we get them repainted. Should be back in place in a few days. In the meantime, there's a bench out front."

So we headed out to the porch again to enjoy our treat. By now the girls faced the street again and pretended not to notice us.

Rosella rolled Eduardo to the right side of the door beside a tiny table and parked her purse under the only other seat, a single fold-up chair that didn't look like it belonged to the ice cream store at all.

"I wish we had another chair," Rosella said. She stepped over to the girls with a smile. "Excuse me. Would you ladies mind if Coral sits with you?"

After all, their seat was as long as the whole front of the store.

They pasted on syrupy smiles. "Sure," the one on the left said. The other one copied her.

But as soon as Rosella turned her back, they looked at each other, snickered, and stared back at me as if I was a reject.

I'd experienced this kind of behavior in the school cafeteria before, and in other places when the teachers weren't watching.

I sat as close to the right end of the bench, and as far away from them as I could. By now their cones were almost gone. Immediately, they edged away and slipped off the side of the porch. From down on the gravel, they glanced back at me over their shoulders, whispered, and giggled as they walked away.

My face burned. What was wrong with me?

Rosella had noticed their behavior as well. She brought Eduardo's chair over to my bench and sat down beside me, creating a little triangle. It was all I could do not to cry.

She wrapped an arm around my shoulders. "Honey, I'm so sorry. Those were extremely rude children. I didn't realize they would act like that, or we wouldn't have stayed. Will you forgive me?"

I hung my head and leaned against her, pinching my nose with the napkin to keep from crying, but the tears came anyway. My shoulders shook. My cone wasn't so appealing now. Rosella caressed my hair and kissed the top of my head. Eduardo took my hand and closed his eyes as if to say he understood.

I never wanted to see those girls again.

But I knew it was more than just the girls' rudeness.
It was my ratty clothes.

Chapter 8

I mentioned nothing about the clothes. Rosella didn't either.

But she understood.

A week or so later we were out on another walk. "Get ready. We're going to stop in at my favorite fabric store," she said, "and you're going to help me pick out some fabric. If it's alright with you and your mom, I'd like to make you a school dress. Think you'd like to learn to sew?"

Fabric store? Sew? I nodded. Over the last several weeks Rosella had taught me how to bake cookies and special secrets about it, like always using shiny pans. We'd made several different recipes by now, and for the first time I was enjoying math, like measuring and doubling the batches. Fractions all made sense now, and by the time school started again, fractions and measuring would be a breeze.

But *sewing?* Mama couldn't teach me. She couldn't even fix the rips in my shirts.

Rosella paused in front of the double glass doors and swept her hand down her side like a model demonstrating a beautiful gown. "I make all my own clothes, you know."

Eduardo grinned his approval at her reflection.

She thought *I* could learn all that?

"You don't buy your dresses at fancy stores?"

"Not a one."

I took her elbow, and we pushed Eduardo through the automatic doors.

If Rosella thought I could learn it, then I could.

Inside of *Yard and Yards* was a maze of color. Cloth everywhere. My eyes widened as, even from the doorway I took in the riot of wildly colored fabrics cascading along every aisle. I could hardly wait to explore.

Eduardo pointed, directing us to the windows where he wanted us to park his chair next to a row of chairs and another man who sat napping with his arms crossed and a puzzle book in his lap. I imagined he, like Eduardo, was also waiting on his wife who was lost somewhere in those wondrous passageways of cloth.

Rosella and I stepped down the first row. "Feel the fabric," she said. Her excitement bubbled over. "Run your hands along the rows. Touch it all."

Amazing. I'd never been in a store like this. "People really make things from all this?" There were wedding gown fabrics and stretchy dance fabrics—shimmery, sparkly, and see-through—everything beautiful under the sun.

She laughed and circled around to the next aisle.

"Come see these." On this aisle were Hawaiian prints with big splashy flowers.

"Just like *your* clothes," I said and gazed at her face. Without a doubt she had spoken the truth about making her own things.

I fingered one of the prints. "It's just like Heaven here," I said. "Why hasn't Mama brought me here before?" I couldn't help but wonder aloud.

She brought me up short. "Does your mama sew?" Her voice had a slight edge to it.

I shrugged.

"Then, please don't criticize her. She probably doesn't know a thing about all this."

From then on I'd keep my thoughts to myself. At least about Mama. But I wished she was more like Rosella. I *wished, wished, wished.*

She quickly changed the subject. "Show me which print you like. Do you have a favorite color?" I guess I was out of the doghouse.

Maybe I was conceited, but I liked coral. Like my name. "Pink," I said. Close enough.

She pulled out several rolls of fabric, or *bolts*, as she called them, with a lot of big, pink flowers. "Let's start by picking two designs."

Designs. I liked that word. I mouthed it beneath my breath, savored it. *Designs.*

"How can I choose? They're all so great."

"Just think. Which two can you *not* leave the store without?"

That simplified things. Shedding my hesitation, I selected a pair, and we put the big rolls she called *bolts* in the shopping cart.

She left me at a table flipping through pattern books and said she was going to find a tape measure. *Wow.* As if the fabrics weren't enough, the beautiful gowns, dresses, and outfits made my head swim. I couldn't get enough.

She returned. "Put a marker in the book, and stand up for me," she said. And right in the middle of the aisle, she proceeded to measure my chest, waist, hips, my arms, my waist to my knees, and even my wrists. "Now we'll find a pattern for you. Can you wear shorts to school? How about sundresses?"

I nodded. "Most anything."

I returned to my book while she flipped through another. Before long she wrote down some numbers. After some rummaging through some metal drawers, she held up an envelope. "Here it is."

I stared at the girls in the illustration, one in a dress and one in shorts. If I could dress like that then kids wouldn't scoot away from me in the cafeteria or at ice cream stores.

"What do you think?"

"Perfect for this hot weather, but..." I hesitated—looked up at her. "No Hawaiian flowers?"

She smiled. "This is just the pattern—a design."

That word again.

"It shows the cut of the clothes. The pattern. But we can use whatever fabric we choose. Every dress or pair of shorts can be different."

"I love it." I glanced at Rosella's smiling face behind the envelope. I couldn't get over the fact that someone actually cared—and was making me a dress. Mama never took me shopping, let alone asked me what I liked. She just brought things home and tossed them at me. "Make it fit," she'd say. "It was free." Castoffs from her restaurant friends. The items frequently had spots or tears. And forget me saying so out loud.

Right now, I was ready to leave, to go back to Rosella's and get started.

"Not so fast. We have to buy notions."

That's when I learned about matching thread, zippers, and bindings.

Once again, I figured we were ready to go.

But we had to wait our turn at the cutting table where she told the salesclerk how much to cut.

"Now listen," she said, leaning close. "I'm getting extra fabric. Before we make this for you, we're going to make a little something for your mother. I don't want her to think badly of me. Understand?"

I nodded.

"And—I'll cut a dress for me out of this same material. That way I'll have leftovers. Remnants."

I nodded. What did leftovers have to do with anything?

"That way, when I ask her if it would be alright to make you something out of remnants, it will feel natural and won't make her feel bad."

Once again, I nodded, even though I didn't completely understand. Whatever Rosella said was okay with me. But Mama never felt bad about anything.

"I know you don't get it. But trust me, I understand about mamas," she said. "And they don't want someone else taking over. Now answer me this. Do you have a dining room table?"

"We eat at the coffee table in front of the couch."

"Okay, that'll work. How big is the table?"

I showed her.

She nodded. "You love your mama, don't you?"

"Of course."

"Then let's surprise her."

Chapter 9

Out in the cabana and seated behind her dark pink Brother sewing machine, she paused as she readied the equipment for my first sewing lesson. "They've got the Heroes Club. This'll be our Girls' Club."

I nodded. "Sounds great to me."

Then she taught me my first lesson on how to thread the machine.

In the meantime, Eduardo pretty much left us alone. It wasn't that he never came out to the cabana. He absolutely did. But he came at random times to work on his jewelry-making hobby, and not too often. It was similar to the way I played cards with the Heroes Club, only a few times a week.

Rosella kept me pretty busy.

The sewing lessons were great fun. And Rosella claimed I was a natural. Within a few days we finished two beautiful Hawaiian placemats for Mama.

Rosella claimed I took to the sewing machine like an *otter in the water*. I couldn't help but grin, so proud of my work. After only a little practice my stitches grew straight and consistent at five-eighths of an inch from the edges. She also taught me how to finish by zig-zagging along raw edges.

There was plenty more to learn, according to her, and I was eager to find out what it was.

"One thing at a time, though," Rosella would say.

She helped me roll up the placemats and tie them with a ribbon. I thought I knew how to tie bows, but she showed me how to make them extra beautiful.

Along with the placemats she packaged up some cookies in a

gift bag with their own decorative bow. I took them to our trailer, laid them on the coffee table, and settled on the couch with a book and some pillows to wait for Mama.

She was going to love her presents.

Night came, and I fell asleep. The next thing I knew Mama was slapping at my legs again, waking me up.

I eased my eyelids open in the dim light, and once again, there she stood, swaying and tottering and bathing me in alcohol breath.

The front door gaped, allowing in the sharp swish of cars passing by on the street. She pointed to the open door. "Go on, Coral. Go on ou'side. We're gonna have some 'dult con-conva-shashun."

Only then did a hulk-sized silhouette manifest in the door frame, courtesy of the streetlight out front.

Uh-oh. I hoped it wasn't that biker guy, that *hiney-pincher.*

I rubbed my eyes and unfolded my legs, knocking my forgotten book onto the floor. I rescued it and slipped it next to the pile where we kept our folded blankets. This time I extracted my bedroll, remembering not to leave without it. If I had to go outside, at least I'd make myself comfortable among the tree roots.

The man's feet scraped against the concrete blocks out front. His bear-sized body rose to block even more of the light. He ducked and entered. It *was* the biker guy. The stink of his alcohol and sour armpits overpowered the room.

"Imunna go t'th bathroom," Mama said.

That left me alone with the beast.

He wasted no time. As soon as Mama's door snapped shut, he moved in my direction with a nasty grin. "My, my, my. If it ain't mah lil' girlie."

A pounding hammered inside my chest. Breathing grew difficult.

My knees wobbled as I backed away. I threw my pallet at him. It dropped in a wad between us. He kicked it aside. Violated my personal space. It all happened so quick. Had he planned this? Worst of all had Mama planned this?

She couldn't have.

Could she?

He raised a massive forearm, and with no effort at all—*Oomph!* He flattened my shoulders against the back door.

I was trapped. A gorilla-size paw tugged at my clothes.

I shot some spit in his face.

Most of it missed. I writhed and squirmed.

"Mama!" A half-whisper was all I could manage.

No answer from her, of course.

He wallowed his mouth in my hair.

Yuck! I leaned away.

My right hand, half-pinned, fell short of the knob. I gritted my teeth and raked my nails across his hand. "Get off me."

He grunted. "Slow down, little lady."

I spat again.

He twisted away. My left hand crossed my body—I had to reach that knob.

But no dice.

His fingers crawled up my leg. I squirmed left and then right.

Jabbed with my elbow.

He grunted. Adjusted his arm.

His grip was like iron. But he was drunk. That had to count for something.

I tried to raise my knee. No room.

So I slackened—and dropped like a rag doll—but *Uch!* No good. He snatched me back up and slammed me against the door—this time by the neck. I couldn't even whisper.

But my shoulders were free.

Come on out, Mama! Help me.

My eyes bulged. Stars flickered behind them.

I tried for the knob.

Twisted it left. Right.

Nothing.

Locked. What a time for that.

His nose touched my own. Hot breath dampened my face. Black devil eyes stared into mine.

I couldn't breathe. His arm tightened. Choked off my air.

He's killing me.
Pain seared my windpipe. The lights in my head grew dim.
I fumbled. Found the latch.
Click.
I gripped the knob.
Twisted. *Click.*
I gulped in air and shoved all at the same time—away from the hairy gorilla—and dangled, kicking, over the blackness below.

Parapet, the angel, extended his arms to break the girl's fall and then stood between her and her attacker.

Prayers from up the coast had opened this mission for the angel.

If only more people would petition their Creator…

The knob slid away. I dropped into the blackness. What else could I do? Weeds broke my fall. I rolled, spinning and flipping and twirling down the steep bank and braced for impact. Weeds scratched and scraped everywhere, and then there was the stream down there at the bottom filled with frogs and snakes and critters, but I wouldn't stay long enough to touch them. I'd jump right back out of that water before they found me.

I landed in the water and leapt to my feet panting and scrambling back up out of there, and all the time my eyes were glued to that trailer and the monster with his head stuck out the back door.

I brushed at the sticks and mud and leaves stuck to my arms. My neck ached—and I stared up at how high the back door was. Of course, I'd known it was high. But from down here it seemed like eight or twelve feet. It's a wonder I hadn't broken my neck.

Parapet stood between Coral and the trailer and lifted his hand in front of the evil man's eyes.

Then out of the corner of my eye—I caught a flicker. Below the door. I froze and stared hard into the space between me and it.

Nothing.

Nothing but the monster-man's shaved head poking out up there.

I clung to the shadows and as silently as possible climbed sideways toward Rosella's bamboo thicket.

The monster's voice called after me. "Where'd you go, honey? Come back here to papa."

No way. I wouldn't have a papa like that. I was pretty sure he couldn't see me now. Or hear me. But would he dare jump?

I crept upward.

"C'mon now, I ain't gonna hurtcha."

I hated living in this dangerous place.

Once again the truth was clear—Mama didn't give a hoot about what happened to me.

As soon as I passed out of sight of that door, I scrambled for all I was worth toward Rosella's place. By now I was shaking all over and bawling as I threw myself against Rosella's door and pounded away.

Next door at Mama's the motorcycle roared to life and sped away into the distance as if chased. Inside Rosella's trailer Yap Yap barked like crazy. The front lights flicked on and Rosella peeked out the door. One glance at me and she swung it open to pull me inside. Her arms encircled me as she squeezed me tight.

"There, there, Coral. I've got you, baby. It's okay. It's okay. Everything's going to be all right."

She held me close until I settled down. Yap Yap danced around us as we made our way to the couch. Then he jumped up between us and climbed onto my lap licking me all over the chin and cheeks like some long-lost friend. He finally settled down and curled up in my arms.

After a bunch of questions to make sure I was alright and my only damage was from the roll down the hill, Rosella herself finally relaxed and began bandaging up my scrapes and prying more details out of me. I told her all of it. And there we sat on the couch, with her stroking my hair, the dog wrapped tight in my arms, and my

toes wedged between the cushions. I eventually fell asleep with my head on her lap.

The next morning, I woke with a pillow under my head and a blanket over me. The sun was up, and it was probably closer to lunch than breakfast. Yap Yap was gone, and neither Eduardo or Rosella were anywhere around. Her hat with its big green flower lay on the table, so she hadn't taken a walk or left me behind. So I waited.

Within minutes the front door opened, and Rosella, in her leafy tropical print, stepped inside.

I sat up as she closed the door behind her.

"You're awake. How are you feeling?"

I shrugged, not sure how to answer.

"Don't worry, honey. He's gone."

The nightmare of what had happened last night came back fresh and raw. "I've got to go back to the trailer," I told her. "Mama doesn't know I'm here."

"Your mama and I had a little talk."

"Is she mad?"

"Mad? Of course not. But I am. I'm not putting up with this kind of thing. No, ma'am."

"You're mad at *me*?"

"Honey, nobody is mad at you. Don't you even think that. What that man did is awful, and we're going to see to it that it doesn't happen again."

Good, she wasn't mad, and Mama wasn't mad.

"But I made a little phone call, and we'll be having some company. A policeman."

My mouth flew open. She held up one hand. "Don't worry. You'll only have to answer a few questions. Tell the officer what you told me last night. Can you do that?"

My trembling started up again, I couldn't help it, and it shook my whole body, but I nodded. The tears welled up and burned as I blinked them away.

"Don't worry. You're not in trouble. The police are on your side. Against the bad guy. I want you to know, though, I didn't say anything about your mama drinking. *This* time."

The policewoman was nice. She smiled and gave me a teddy bear with a big pink bow on its neck. I gave it a big squeeze. Her visit was nothing like I feared.

She asked easy questions, like what he said and I said and what he did and what I did, and where was Mama when it happened. I told her Mama was in the bathroom but followed Rosella's lead and skipped the part about her being drunk.

Still, I was glad when her questions were over. She put away her pencil and notebook and told me how proud she was of me and that I was smart and did the right thing by running over to Rosella's. She also said they would find the man, and he shouldn't be coming around again.

Rosella then repeated to the policewoman what she already told me, that I could come over to her house at any time, day or night.

The policewoman moved as if to stand but asked me if there was anything else I wanted to tell her before she said good-bye.

I said no. But there was one strange thing. And I left it out on purpose. Because it wouldn't matter to her, and she'd think I was lying or crazy.

All over the place behind Mama's trailer and beside the bamboo, the air had smelled perfumy—like roses.

But there were no roses back there. Or anywhere around that I knew of.

So I left that part out.

After she stood, she walked out front with Rosella.

I stayed inside. Through the half-closed door little bits and pieces of their discussion filtered in. I shouldn't have been listening in, but Rosella said something about DCF and a foster license, and could they help her expedite things.

I wasn't sure what *DCF* was, or the other things.

But that same morning when we took our walk, we visited the DCF office.

Chapter 10

Eduardo was already waiting out by the mosaic table as I finished my breakfast at their kitchen table. He had been reading his newspaper. It was late morning and the usual time for the Heroes Club. But after my attack last night today was different. The gate was shut.

Eduardo gave me a big wonderful smile and kissed the back of my hand like he was amazed to see me. He couldn't say it, but his face and all his actions said, "I love you."

I grinned. "I love you, too. *Grandpa.*" He couldn't really argue with me. If I *did* have a grandpa, I'd want him to be just like Eduardo. It was the first time I ever called him that, and he squeezed my hand with both of his. I guess he liked being called Grandpa.

We headed out the front gate but took a different route downtown that day—past a vacant school—and arrived at a large brick and glass building. A blue Florida map decorated its glass doors. Underneath it in gray were the big letters *DCF.* An arc of words above that said *Florida Department of Children and Families.* I pushed open the door and held it for Rosella and Eduardo.

"Thank you. Now please wait over there with Eduardo," she said, pointing to a row of chairs by the wall.

I may have been over to the side, but I kept a good eye on her since this had something to do with me. She spoke to a lady at the desk who gave her some papers to fill out. After that, she moved and sat across the desk from another lady, where they talked some more, and Rosella took lots of notes.

A few words filtered over to me. That word *expedite* and something else about afternoon classes. This was summer vacation, and I had no desire for that.

After the meeting I asked Rosella about the classes.

"My goodness, you have good hearing," she said. "Don't worry, though. *I'm* the one to take the classes."

She mentioned something about a license and that it would take a few months. She didn't explain why she was doing it.

That day we ate lunch out. Rosella took us to a restaurant she called a diner. It looked like a train. The only other restaurant I'd ever been to was a McDonald's or Burger King. But this was better.

A few days later Rosella told me she made some kind of deal with Mama. Something about a scholarship.

Again, it sounded like school, so I didn't like it.

Pretty soon, though, I learned it had nothing to do with school. And that was the first time I ever heard of summer camp.

Looking back on that summer, there were changes, but none I could put my finger on or explain. And many I didn't notice for a long time after.

First, Rosella didn't seem to be very concerned anymore about making Mama happy, or getting her approval for things. She seemed to be in charge.

Another important change, I only gradually realized. For some reason, from that time until I was fourteen, Mama and I never moved again.

Chapter 11

Aweek or so after that trip to downtown, checkers day came around, and the Heroes Club was a man down. That meant they'd have to change to cards or some other game if I didn't join in.

"Why don't you play checkers with them?" Rosella said. "At least for a little while."

As we spoke the mail arrived with a letter for Rosella—one she seemed very interested in. She stood there in the yard reading it, then disappeared over at Mama's. I decided to go ahead and play checkers with my friends. After a bit she returned as if nothing had happened and served coffee and cookies to the group. This time she wouldn't let me help.

"Enjoy yourself. The carpenter's coming, so you stick around out here, today, okay?

Carpenter? I was dying to go inside with her and find out what she and Mama talked about. "But what did…?"

"We discussed something," was all I could get out of her. So I stayed outside and forgot about it. My heroes may have let me win a couple of games, but I didn't let on. But on the other hand, maybe I'd actually improved.

The carpenter did not appear. In the meantime, the games ended, and the men returned to their homes. Lunch came and went. Rosella and I sat around inside reading books while Eduardo went in the bedroom and took his nap. Yap Yap went with him.

Finally came the knock on the door.

"Mr. O'Malley," Rosella said as she opened the door. She kept her voice low since Eduardo was asleep. "Come in. Thanks for coming on such short notice. Coral, this is the man who built our cabana."

"Very nice to meet you," I said, remembering my manners. He carried a tool box in one hand and a wad of knotted rope under his arm.

"So," he said, acknowledging me with a nod. He turned back to Rosella who handed him the letter she'd gotten in the mail. I still had no idea what it said.

"Wanna show me where you want this here thing?" he said.

"What's he going to make?" I whispered.

She ignored my curiosity and whispered to me it was something good, but I needed to stay inside and read until the man left.

She led him out the back door. "Follow me."

I couldn't see or hear a thing. So I did as she said and found a good book.

After he left, Rosella came and got me. We walked around between the trailer and the shed and stood underneath the cabana. It was the first time I'd been down there in her back yard. A rope ladder hung down between two bird of paradise plants. "Climb on up," she said.

More than happy to comply. I scrambled right up. "Woo hoo! Now what?" I yelled down from the top. I felt like a pirate in a ship.

"Leave it there and find that other rope. It's there behind the post."

I found it.

"Unwind it and swing back down."

I found this task a little bit trickier than climbing up. There was nowhere on the rope to grip.

"Okay," Rosella said. "I'll tie a few knots in it and we'll practice later. Climb back down the best way you can."

I chose the ladder. "Ahoy, matey," I said, jumping off at the bottom and saluting her. I didn't care if I *did* sound like a little kid. She laughed, and we strolled across the white sand under the cabana. Somehow the space below didn't seem as big as the cabana above. We stepped behind the building to the bank of the stream that meandered behind the trailer park. It wasn't very deep, but probably had some good minnows and critters. I'd never really explored it. Not yet, anyway.

"Why not climb up the ladder and swing down the rope—try to strengthen your hands."

I could imagine having a rope or rope ladder up in one of these trees over the stream. And the vines—they'd be fun to explore. Maybe I'd be able to see over the roof.

I decided to come back later and explore the stream below as we returned to the ladder.

She reached around behind a support beam and found a skinny cord. "Watch this." She gave it a hard pull and the ladder rose into the air. It gathered in a clump near the roofline. She wrapped the cord around a cleat on the post. "If you ever need to climb and get away from some maniac, unwind the cord and let down the ladder. Once you get upstairs, pull the cord in behind you and wrap it around a cleat up there. The single rope for down. The ladder for up. Easy?"

I nodded.

"Now, Coral, tell me. We both know you're too big to be playing pirates, so why in the world did I have Mr. O'Malley put up this rope and ladder?"

I sucked in a breath. "For..." I studied her face, hoping it was the one thing I needed in the whole world.

"...me?"

She nodded. "It's your get-away ladder. From..."

"The biker-guys?" My voice fairly squeaked.

"Yes ma'am."

She led me through the house again, and I sighed from relief as I followed. How did she always know? Back in the cabana she added big knots to the single rope and looped it around its cleat. "This is how you get away in a hurry."

I nodded. "Got it."

My hand slid along the railing. Tears had been working their way up, and I leaned against her, bawling. "Thank you, Rosella, thank you so much. How did you know? How did you *know*? I was so scared."

"Now, now, now. Let's get you a tissue." She kissed me on the forehead and led me through the kitchen where she snatched a paper towel off the roll.

I wiped the snot and tears from my face as she kept on. "Think of your ropes as fun. You can practice on them all you like. But I won't have you hiding under that tree anymore in the middle of the night. You come straight over here."

I sniffed. "Okay," I said, but it came out all warbly.

"I'm an old lady. There may come a time I can't hear what's going on. And you'll need a place to go. I'm not trying to scare you. You already know the dangers."

She pointed to the back left corner of the cabana. "There's your getaway room. It's unlocked. But it *does* lock from the inside."

Getaway room?

She led me to its door and pushed it open.

My mouth dropped open.

A white twin bed, with a pink ruffled bedspread and pillow filled half the room. The other half held a pink rug, a desk with a lamp, a phone, and a straight-backed chair. Pink ruffled curtains covered its single window.

Rosella watched my face. "Go on in." Her voice choked.

I stepped across the matching rug. It was as fuzzy as a stuffed toy. I wanted to take off my shoes and run my toes through it.

"Open that door on the right," she said, nodding toward one of two in the back. I hadn't even noticed.

Behind it was a tiny pink bathroom with its own pink rug and matching towel.

I glanced at the other door.

"Never mind about that one," she said. "It's just an old storage closet. But here's what's important. This room is where you'll hide the next time you have to run away. Climb the rope and come on in."

A place to hide. I turned all the way around as the dream sank in.

"But—how will you know I'm out here?"

She yanked a few times on a long ribbon hanging from the ceiling near the bed. "There's your bell. It connects to my trailer. Pull and pull and pull until I hear it." She opened a drawer. "Here's a walkie talkie. I'll teach you how to use it."

All this talk and preparation made me antsy and a little nervous. Maybe scared. And very happy. So much was happening. I wanted to get down to the stream and wrap my mind around it. Let it sink in. I wanted to sit in the sand with my feet in the water. And think.

But it would wait.
And what I soon discovered would lead me in another direction.

53

Chapter 12

Rosella became my hero in so many ways. The bullies at the ice cream shop had dug a scar across my heart. Rosella had never said a thing about my torn or shabby clothes. But she knew, and I knew that she did. And without making me ashamed, she taught me ways to solve the problem.

It was late morning, and the Heroes Club was in full swing outside. Yap Yap was out there too, claiming his territory on Eduardo's lap. Anytime the little squirt escaped out the door, he would race to Eduardo's chair and dance around his elbows until he picked him up and held him in his lap. First and foremost, he was Eduardo's dog and stayed with him most of the time.

Rosella and I had finished cleaning the kitchen and were sitting in the living room taking turns reading jokes to each other from our joke books. "A laugh a day makes the blues go away," Rosella liked to say. At night, she told me she read grown-up jokes to Eduardo from the *Readers' Digest* and made sure they watched at least one *I Love Lucy* or *Red Skelton Show* from the old days. She kept a big DVD collection.

Rosella laid her joke book aside and gave me a smile. "Coral, I've got a few items that need fixing. Some mending. Would you like to help me? You'll learn some new sewing tricks."

She'd just completed two Hawaiian outfits for me from her leftovers. I was ready and willing to help her with anything. "Sure."

In fact, she still had scraps from that project, and I wanted to make some clothes for Yap Yap. I just hadn't told her my idea yet.

And doll clothes. I wanted to make gowns and wedding dresses if I could get my hands on a Barbie doll.

I glanced around at the starched curtains in her living room and at the tablecloth in her little kitchen. Nothing in her house was ever torn. "What needs fixing?"

She patted a stack of un-ironed laundry on top of the hassock. On top lay her pink Hawaiian dress, my favorite. She picked it up and showed me the hem. "This is half torn-out."

"I want to learn all the tricks," I said. "I love to sew."

The only thing I'd made so far was that pair of placemats for Mama. But I'd seen Rosella at work. She'd made me clothes and sewed her own using a dress form out in the cabana. It's like a giant doll-body that she tries her outfits on.

If I could only dream up new designs and make them like Rosella did.

Designs.

One day I'd have my own dress form like hers.

"Hand-sewing is not the same as machine sewing. But it's not complicated. You already know how to match the thread, so let's start by threading a needle."

That morning I learned blind hem-stitching, whose invisible stitches I fell in love with. Maybe I could be invisible to Mama's creepy boyfriends.

Then after a few knotty starts, Rosella taught me to sew buttons on Eduardo's shirt. "Just like the pioneers did in historic times," she said. "Did you know they made their own buttons?"

"Can we do that?" I said.

"What? Make buttons?" She just smiled. "Someday, maybe. I never thought of doing it."

We finished the mending—some of it hers and some of it Eduardo's. "Well, that's all I have," she said, and we packed away the sewing equipment in her fancy sewing basket that I'd admired as we worked—a pink and white basket with satin tufting for needles and pins and a matching handle. A nested tray fit under the lid and held little things like thimbles, scissors, and thread. Below it was a space for folded fabrics and packages of zippers or binding.

"I love your basket," I said. "I've never seen one before."

"Very handy." She held up the basket. "Just pack up your sewing and carry it from room to room."

"Like you said, 'everything is in its own little place.'" I thought about the way we lived at home, all tossed and tumbled, stacked and crammed, and I hated it.

"I wish I had more things to mend," I told her.

Rosella just smiled.

I did have more things—at home. My clothes were a mess with missing buttons, ripped seams and hems. I knew how to fix them now. Up until today I could only cover up the flaws with an arm or a book. And judging by the ice-cream shop girls, that plan wasn't working.

But I didn't have a sewing box or needles, or thread, or anything such as that at home. "Do you think I could... Could I bring over some mending tomorrow?"

Her smile warmed my heart. "Of course, you can. Bring over whatever you like. And if there's some new trick to learn, we'll figure it out together."

I could hardly wait. I'd never be ashamed again.

Rosella.

Thinking back years later, she'd probably planned the whole thing.

Anyway, the next day, not only did we fix clothes, Rosella had a surprise idea.

Chapter 13

Wed set out for our morning walk, and left Yap Yap at home
as usual. Unless Eduardo carried him. Rosella thought it was too
far for his little Yorkie legs. He'd get too tired.

I skipped ahead, thrilled with my new Hawaiian outfit she'd
made me. But Rosella, very spry for someone her age, always pushed
Eduardo along at a pretty fast pace, and was never far behind.

I wanted to be just like her when I got old.

Besides my new outfit, I sported a new necklace and bracelet
that Eduardo had made me from tiny white shells off Sanibel
Island Beach.

Made them for *me*.

He'd made one for Mama, too. I felt like a million dollars, and
she would too.

"Something for you—and always something for your mama,"
Rosella would say, like she wanted to make things equal between
us. She'd done the same thing with Mama's cookies and placemats,
but that seemed so long ago now.

"Ahem ... I've got a surprise for you, Coral."

I reverse-walked, facing Rosella, "What? Tell me."

Her eyes twinkled. Eduardo nodded and grinned like he was
in on the surprise too.

"Let's talk about it at the ice cream shop."

The air left my chest. I stopped in my tracks.

Oh, no. Not the ice cream shop. I pictured the two girls.

"You can do it, Coral. I bet those girls won't even be there."

Even from here, a block away, I could see its freshly painted
porch furniture and new pink and white awnings. What a change.

But Rosella had been mistaken. There on the bench sat the girls again with their cones. Such bad timing. They must be rich to come here every day.

"Don't dodge them, Coral," Rosella whispered. "Or they win. Walk right in there and pretend you own the place. Give them a big smile. You're a beautiful lady, and very smart compared to them."

Beautiful? Lady? Very?

My knees weakened as we approached. But with no time to think and no ideas of my own, I decided to follow Rosella's instructions. I took a deep breath and strode forward.

"Be sure you say good morning loud and clear," she added, "and when you get to the door swing it open like you're the boss. Remember, *they're* the visitors. And act like you have a happy secret."

I wasn't sure what Rosella meant, and we were almost there. It was too late to back out. I could pretend, though, as well as the next person. As we stepped across the patio, I forced out my cheeriest "Good morning," despite my shakes. Maybe they didn't notice.

Eduardo lifted his hand in greeting to them.

Rosella purred like a movie star. "Good morning, ladies."

The girls, likely confused at the bold turn-around, just stared. One elbowed the other and as soon as we passed, they skedaddled, as if they were afraid. But this time they didn't talk and turn, talk and turn—they just *scrambled away.* I felt like laughing.

What had happened?

Inside the shop Rosella laughed and grabbed me up in a hug. She squeezed me tight. "Way to scare off the bullies! You were great, Coral. Just great! You stood up to them and showed them you weren't going to be their victim."

Trembling all over, I hugged her back.

"I know you were scared. But I'm so proud of you."

Eduardo gripped my hand.

Wow. I'd have to think this over and try it at school.

"Always remember, Coral. They are no better than you. You are no less than them."

Eduardo added a wink and a nod.

"I think this calls for a hot fudge sundae celebration," Rosella said.

Hot fudge sundae? I'd never had one.

But neither the run-in with the girls nor the hot fudge sundae was the surprise Rosella had lined up for me. Nor were her fun plans to start taking me to the Baptist church on Sundays. Or the newspaper writing contest she would have me enter.

Nope. Her big surprise had something to do with me saving money.

A thing I did not have. Not one red cent.

Chapter 14

We ate our ice-cream-shop sundaes indoors this time, seated on the newly painted curlicued chairs and admiring all the new wall-art and posters. When we were done, we tossed our trash in their pink can.

If I knew anything about Rosella, she liked this ice cream shop for its colors and decor.

I liked it too.

Outside on the porch, I returned her hug. "Thank you, Rosella. That was the best sundae in the world."

"You're very welcome," she said as I let go and skipped across the parking lot to wait for them on the corner.

They caught up, and we turned left.

Rosella grinned. "You know, Eduardo, I think we'll head back to the fabric store this morning. What do you say?"

His nod and wink told me something was up.

More clothes?

My skipping resumed as I led the way.

Great. I loved surprises.

Inside the fabric shop we parked Eduardo by the front window again. Shopping wasn't his thing. He pulled a crossword puzzle and pen from the chair's side pocket and shooed us away.

This time Rosella guided me straight to the shelves with the... *sewing baskets?*

My mouth flew open. I hadn't explored this aisle before. The baskets were all so beautiful—every color of the rainbow, every size imaginable.

"I know you liked mine, but how would you like to earn one of your own?"

Earn? Speechless, I nodded. "How?" was all I could manage.

She pointed toward the pattern tables where we'd sat before. "Pick out the one you like and meet me over there."

I slid out a solid pink basket about the size and look of hers and lifted out its tray. It had the same silken lining as Rosella's.

I shut it back and brought it to the table. She'd barely had time to sit down. "Goodness. That didn't take long at all."

"This one. It's my favorite color."

"You sure this is the one?"

I hugged it to my chest. "Yes," I whispered, as if the deal would go away if I said it too loud. "This is the one."

But how would I ever earn such a thing?

"All right, then. Have a seat."

Rosella pulled out a little notebook. "How this works is you'll do work for me which counts as money. Like a job. Are you interested?"

I pressed my lips together and gave her a firm nod. Work didn't scare me. I had no other resources.

"Margot owns this store, and she's agreed to help us. She'll place your basket in the back room with your name on it. It's called layaway. Once you've earned the right amount, you can come down and pay it off."

"Could—when I earn it, I mean—could I keep it at your house?" I was concerned about what might happen to it over at Mama's house. I spent most of my days at Rosella's anyway.

"Of course." Rosella wrote down the price of the sewing basket. "There's a 6.5% sales tax." She helped me figure and add that in to find the total. "When we get home, we'll sit down and figure out your jobs."

I fixed my eyes on this dear little lady, and then leaped up to give her the biggest hug ever. How did I deserve her in my life? "Rosella, you are so perfect. I think you're the most wonderful person in the whole world."

She patted my back and rocked me back and forth. "No, no, no. Not perfect, little one." She pulled my head down and kissed it on top. "If you only knew. If you only knew."

I won the writing contest and entered many more over the years. Rosella had helped me zero in on my talents. It was scary to think what would have happened to me if she hadn't come out and found me that night.

Another change began to happen that summer, and it went on for years. And this one helped me find more topics to write about. After the biker guy episode, Rosella began paying my scholarship to a variety of summer camps. She wanted me to be well-rounded. Sometimes camp lasted for one week, like that first summer, and sometimes two. There were critter camps, sewing camps, beach camps, going-back-in-time camps, science camps, art camps, and sports camps. She always let me choose.

It was the week before camp that second summer that I discovered the small stack of brand-new clothes in her hassock.

Boy clothes.

Chapter 15

Rosella was out in the cabana gathering some cleaning supplies. I was horsing around with Yap Yap in the living room and wondering how Rosella would have me earn my sewing basket. I couldn't tell whether the dog loved or hated her citrus-scented dusting spray, but he growled and grabbed the cloth Rosella had left on the table then darted around the room with it. I tried to get it back, and we ended up playing tug-o'-war on opposite sides of the hassock. I fell across it, and the lid fell off.

"Yap Yap, you little stinker. You made me break it."

But the hassock wasn't broken. And what fell out was a pile of new clothes—shorts, shirts, and shoes, with all the tags still on them. I held up the pants—about my size, only a little bigger.

As quick as lightning, I folded up the things and stuffed them back in, replacing the lid.

What was Rosella doing with boy clothes?

When she returned, I gathered my nerve to ask. "What about those clothes, those boy-clothes?"

She gave me a look that said, *How in the world did you discover those?*

"I promise, I wasn't snooping. Yap Yap and I were playing and the hassock lid fell off."

"Remember what I said about promising."

"Okay, I don't promise, then. But I wasn't snooping."

"That's better. Don't worry. They're not for you. But they *are* for somebody very special like you."

She led me over to the refrigerator and tapped the oily spot on the picture of a pale, balding man which she'd anointed and prayed over so many mornings. There was no way the clothes were for *him*.

"When you pray, Coral, pray for this one lost sheep, that God would save him."

Man. She sure could change the subject.

A sadness crept over her features. I watched her face and thought about the balding man in the picture—what could he possibly have to do with those clothes?

"This is Sol Flores. My son. And until God does a miracle, his heart is as black as a lump of coal."

I started to say, *I promise,* but caught myself. "I will, Rosella. Every night." In fact, I needed to start my own list.

"And I believe you will." She hugged me to her side. "Thank you,' she whispered.

After that, no matter how I begged, the only thing Rosella would say about the boy's clothes was it was part of that *grief,* and one day she'd explain a little more.

Pretty soon I came across a second mystery.

Chapter 16

Later that day, Rosella and I pored over the contents of our newly arrived camp literature at the kitchen table. Spread over the table were all the papers we needed for Sanibel Science Camp, a Baptist-sponsored affair that I couldn't wait to experience: receipt of registration, itinerary, and packing instructions.

Camp was coming soon, ready or not.

My hands trembled as I followed Rosella's instructions checking off soap, towels, and other things she said we already had. She scribbled a list on her own notepad of things we still needed.

"We'll get you a new toothbrush, toothpaste, *girls' club* toiletries of your own...*and,*" she added, tapping me on the nose, "new underwear!" I grinned, and we burst out giggling. How could she know? How could she possibly know I needed underwear—and those other things I couldn't even mention—listed as *personal items* on the camp list—the kind I'd snitched from Mama every month, and we never talked about.

Rosella patted my hand and kept writing.

How I wished Rosella was my real grandma. Nobody's grandma could be smarter or kinder than Rosella.

I made another check. Then it hit me. "What about a suitcase?"

She tipped her head, frowned, and then looked at me sideways. Some kind of big decision was going on inside her head. It took a long minute, but she spread her fingers on the table and rose with a heavy sigh. "All right. Come on. If we must, we must. I think the time has come."

The time has come? There must be more to this than simply finding a suitcase. Butterflies stirred in my stomach.

That day was a Tuesday. I'll never forget. Rosella in her red, and me in my equally bright capris she'd made me.

Inside the cabana, she paused with her hand on the knob of my get-away room. An unhappy dread seemed to cloud her face. She sighed and turned the knob. I followed her inside.

One hand flicked on the lamp, and the other fanned the air. "Whew. Stuffy in here." She crossed the room and pushed a button on the air conditioning unit.

Whatever the big deal was, she was taking her time. Or stalling.

The window unit groaned and shuddered, delivering a loud vibrating roar that took over the room. Rosella ignored the noise and stepped to the back of the room to the narrow accordion closet she'd once called "just a storage closet."

She drew it open and stood to the side. Observing me.

A gasp flew out of my mouth. Never mind the plain black suitcase down in the bottom right corner.

Sequins and satins filled the closet. Fancy gowns. They cascaded from hangers and shimmered in the low light. A rainbow of feather boas hung from hooks on the left. Dozens of glittering high heels lined the floor. Others peeked out from the shoe bags.

I fingered the materials. *"Rosella...*it's like a millionaire's closet. Where did these come from?"

She clamped her lips together and reached an arm around my shoulder.

"It was a long time ago. Another life. And I'm not proud."

She stepped toward the bed and sat. "Have a seat," she said, patting the pink bedspread beside her. Her eyes held mine as I tore myself away from the spectacle and stepped toward her.

"I hope you won't be too disappointed at what I'm going to tell you."

My eyes drifted back to the closet as I squiggled beside her.

"You've thought so highly of me, Coral. But I..."

"You're the most wonderful person I've ever met."

She shook her head and nodded toward the dresses. "That's all about to go. But you had to know the truth. You deserve that much. And no, Coral. Nobody is perfect."

"Is this the grief?"

She laughed. "This is the Las Vegas showgirl and all that goes with it. Drinking, smoking. Provoking the men." She lifted her chin toward the closet. "Oh, it looks pretty. Beautiful, even. But it was Death. And it's dead."

Death? Dead?

I wasn't sure I caught on. "But how...?"

She sighed and waited a long minute. "My son. I brought him into this world and traded him in for all this glamour. I sold him out. And he went to pot." She snorted. "Literally."

I frowned, trying to understand. It didn't make sense. Rosella, the perfect teacher, the perfect grandmother to me...

"I destroyed him, Coral. Neglected the socks off him. Right from his very first newborn diaper. And what have I got to show? A ruined son."

"The one you showed me on the refrigerator?" I didn't want to say *bald man.*

She closed her eyes and a look of pain crossed her face as she nodded. "My one and only."

"*Pray* for him," I urged her. "You're always praying for everyone."

Her smile relieved me. She wasn't undone, at least. What would I do if Rosella fell apart?

"I do pray. But I get discouraged now and then," she said. "It's been a long time."

I laid my hand on hers. "He can't be that bad."

"I see others with their normal grown-up sons. But I've never even felt that for one day." She shook her head and snorted. "And I've got no one to blame but myself. He's a greedy, money-hungry stranger to us and wouldn't care if Eduardo and I died today. He'd be holding out his hands demanding the money. Probably have us cremated or better yet, donated to science. It's even cheaper than cremation." She shook her head. "He's going to be in for a little surprise."

"Don't say that." I squeezed her hand, but felt confused. Here I was, a kid encouraging a grown-up. And her reference to science—how strange. Whatever she meant, it wasn't something good. "You've got *me*, though. I can pray for him."

"There's power in two people praying."

"I won't quit until he's changed. I promise." I clamped my hand over my mouth. The word had escaped before I could think.

She kissed my cheek. "Thank you."

My gaze followed her sweet face as she turned away. "Don't worry about me," I told her. I'll never be disappointed in you."

Her wrinkled hand patted my knee, and she exhaled a long, slow breath as if it had been held in. "What do you say we get all this old stuff bagged up and get it donated somewhere?"

I nodded, and we stood.

"Coral," she said. "If Eduardo and I go first, will you keep on reminding God to straighten out my son? You won't quit? Ever? Until it happens?"

I nodded. She'd reminded me so many times that God wanted us to keep pestering Him. Like the widow banging on the judge's door in the middle of the night to wake him up, and she finally got what she wanted.

"I just don't want my son burning in hell."

I couldn't forget him, not with those pictures on the refrigerator.

As an afterthought, she grabbed my hand. "And keep him from cremating us. Can you do that? I want a regular funeral."

Seconds slipped by as I gazed into those earnest blue eyes. I had no idea what cremation was. But there was nothing I wouldn't do for her.

"Of course."

Little did I realize, I'd be losing more folks than Mama that year.

It took us a few hours to fold and cram twenty brown grocery bags full of clothes and shoes and line them up against the rail in the cabana.

"Each day we'll take a bag and stuff it in the Salvation Army box," she said. "I bet they'll be surprised."

It was my turn to sigh. This would take a bunch of walks to town.

Two days later, Rosella and I stood beside her bed with her big suitcase open in front of us. It was mid-June, and we'd nearly finished packing my things for camp. Every item, down to the bug repellant, had been bought and packed in tight—all except the bathing suit. She'd sewn all my other camping clothes, and on the inside, I was jumping up and down, eager to wear them.

"I'm not about to tackle making a bathing suit," she said. "So tomorrow we'll be heading to the store. Be sure to get your mama's permission."

I wouldn't forget it for the world. Our science camp bus would be pulling out of town in two days.

"The trick will be finding a modest one," she said.

I stayed up late that night to make sure I got Mama's permission. A note might get lost or misplaced somehow.

Turned out permission wasn't quite so simple.

"Fine," Mama said, with a toss of her head. She'd definitely had some alcohol, but there were no men outside. "So where's *my* bathing suit?"

Every time Rosella bought or made me something Mama wanted one too. The more Rosella did for Mama, the more demanding Mama became.

I guess Rosella understood her tendencies before I ever did, but I was beginning to realize Mama acted more like another child than a mother. Had she been this childish the whole time?

"I'll let Rosella know," I told her.

"No, no, no. Just kidding. But you could mention I have a birthday coming up on Friday."

How rude. People don't normally go around mentioning their birthday to other people. Not in order to get something. It was also embarrassing. I was embarrassed for me and embarrassed for Mama.

In May Rosella had celebrated my own fourteenth birthday and the end of the school year. She made me a party dress and bought me a real bakery cake with pink roses and one special gift, a long pink nightgown like hers. We'd arranged the party on Mama's day off, but at the last minute, Mama had to work.

Peter, the attorney, and all the heroes came with their fat cigars. Those who had wives brought them.

Darkness fell, and Rosella switched on the twinkly lights and Cuban music, and we all danced under the mango trees and ate *yuca* and *ropa vieja* with rice and beans. After the gifts Rosella served pink ice cream, espresso, and tropical fruit juices to go with the cake. I couldn't stop smiling and blinking back tears.

It was my first birthday cake, my first party dress, and my first party ever.

When Mama came home that night, I took her a big piece of cake, one with roses.

And now it was clear she remembered that cake, and she wanted something too.

I didn't blame her for wanting a cake. But to ask for one?

Right now, I hated being the go-between.

I hung my head and told Rosella what Mama had said. "I'm really sorry," I said.

"Why? Don't be sorry. Trust me. This is an opportunity."

"What do you mean? I thought you'd want to tell Mama off."

"We're going to surprise her."

That morning, Rosella and Eduardo and I headed out to Penney's to find a bathing suit. We settled on a cute sailor style, very modest—a two-piece with a cover-up.

Eduardo carried the shopping bag on his lap, and we headed for the grocery store.

At the greeting card section Rosella put an arm around my shoulders. "Just wait. Your mama is going to be so tickled with her surprises."

Right there in the store, Rosella gave me a lesson on shopping for cards. She pointed out the different sections. "See, pink for girls, blue for boys, and here's the birthday collection. It's as simple as reading. Now find the pockets that say mother." I selected a card, and we headed to the bakery where she guided me through ordering a cake under my own name.

Rosella was determined to teach me some birthday skills.

"I love this," I told her.

She tapped my nose. "It's always fun to do for others."

I'll never forget that cake—yellow with butter cream icing and yellow daisies.

"What message on top?" the baker asked.

I grinned at the hugeness of my privilege. But I didn't have to think hard. *"Happy Birthday, Mama. I love you."*

At the candle rack, I chose a single 2 and 8. Mama was only fourteen when I was born. The same as me now. I couldn't imagine someone having a baby at my age.

"And while we're doing all this," Rosella led me over to the floral section, "let's have you order a couple of helium balloons."

After all that ordering, I felt like a birthday expert.

On the way home Rosella carried the cake—to make sure it didn't get dropped—and had me push Eduardo's wheelchair. I parked Eduardo inside her gate, and she brought the cake all the way to my front door where I took it inside.

Mama wasn't home yet, so we walked back to Rosella's where Eduardo was waiting.

"Tonight, after you light those candles, dunk the match in a cup of water," she said.

"I prom... I will," I assured her. I was scared of fire, too.

I couldn't wait to see Mama's face that night. I listened for her battered Honda as it *sput-sput-sputted* into the yard. Then I grabbed the matches. My hand trembled as I lit the candles before she got in the door. I remembered to dunk the match in water and turned off the lamp. Except for the light of those two candles, the room fell dark. I breathed in the smell of burnt matches and waited.

Mama opened the door. The candles flickered but didn't blow out.

"Happy birthday to you," I sang as they settled back down. "Happy birthday to you, happy birthday, dear Mama, happy birthday to you."

She stood in the open doorway, her face pale in the candlelight and her fingertips against her gaping mouth.

Her glittering eyes never left the cake as she shut the door and made her way to the couch. She sank down beside me. Gazing into the flames, she wrapped an arm around my shoulders. Tears rolled down her face as she shook her head.

I hugged her back. "I love you, Mama."

"I never had one of these," she said, her voice cracking. "It's beautiful. Nobody ever got me a cake."

She'd never told me that before.

I pushed the card into her hands, and she tore it open and read every word. She loved it and leaned against me, sniffling into my hair as she hugged me tight.

I was happy Rosella understood about Mama and so glad she got her cake.

There was no way I could know it that day, but this would be Mama's last birthday.

I adored Baptist science camp. That week at the beach was like heaven. My friends and I caught all kinds of things from the water. We touched them with our hands and learned about God's ocean and its seaside creatures and plants and how wonderful they are and how all of nature works together.

And every evening we found ourselves gazing west into the orange, red, and purple sunsets over the Gulf of Mexico. I would come back to town tanned and happy.

The Gulf wasn't but a few miles away from our place—closer than I'd imagined. I made a lot of new friends, girls from other schools, and we all promised each other we'd see each other again at camp next year, and I hoped I could keep my word.

As great as I loved camp, though, my mind kept drifting back to things at home.

How was I going to earn that pink sewing basket, and what tasks would it take to make it happen?

On Friday afternoon Rosella met our returning camp bus under the carport of the Baptist Church. As we pulled in, all the girls and I craned our necks to peer through the bus windows—they to search for their moms and dads, and I for Rosella.

And there she stood in her orange and yellow dress, just like one of our Gulf of Mexico sunsets. After that whole week away she hadn't forgotten me. She'd remembered to come.

I imagined, by the way all my friends looked out of those bus windows, the rest of them needed that same reassurance, too.

Properly satisfied, we grabbed our things and crowded off the bus, eager to see our loved ones. I bounded off with the rest of my friends. They all bolted for their parents, and I headed for Rosella who wrapped me in a giant hug.

"Mmm, mmmm, mmm," she said, squeezing me tight. "It's so good to have you back, Coral." She leaned away and studied my tanned and grinning face. "Don't you look good! And everybody here at home's just fine, too. All of us, your mom, Eduardo and I, and all the uncles—we missed you so much." She hugged me again, almost smothering me.

My face almost cramped from smiling so hard. "Me too. I missed you all, too."

She helped me roll the suitcase toward the parking lot.

"We're not walking all the way home, are we?" I said, scanning the rows for Peter's familiar car. He'd brought us here a week ago, and always drove us to important places.

His car was nowhere in sight. My suitcase did have rollers, though. "Over there. The black Mustang." She jangled a set of keys.

"Mustang?" I studied the vehicle. I'd never seen it before.

She laughed, obviously enjoying my surprise.

"It can't be yours," I said. "You don't have a car."

Her eyes sparkled as she approached the vehicle and opened the trunk.

"When—where'd it come from?"

We lifted the suitcase in, and I could tell by the amusement on her face she was enjoying my suspense.

"Oh, it's ours. I'll tell you sometime."

"Arrgh!" I sputtered as she slammed the trunk and we climbed in.

"Well...." I ran my hand over the upholstery with its fine black leather, so soft and well-kept. There wasn't a speck of dust or dirt anywhere. "Where have you been keeping it?"

She grinned and shook her head. "Can't tell you right now. Tell me about your camp."

Well, that started it. There was no need for her to ask twice. I pushed aside my curiosity about the car and started in about my week. I yakked all the way back to her place. Of course, it was only a few blocks. But I hardly stopped. There was so much to talk about. She pulled in on the right side of her fence and snugged that car into the shed beside her house. It must have been hiding in there this whole time.

"Wow." I gazed at her with my mouth hanging open. "All this time I thought you had tools in there."

She gave me another grin.

"Every time I turn around, you're surprising me again."

We tugged the suitcase through the front door of the house, down the boardwalk, and out to the cabana where Eduardo waited. I laid it on the floor, zipped it open, and then darted over to give him a big hug around the neck.

"Thank you for letting me go to camp, Eduardo. I know it was from both of you. Thank you so much." He nodded and motioned with his hand for me to speak and tell him about my experience.

I kissed him on top of his head and knelt beside the suitcase to plunder through its wadded contents. "First, I'll show you the stuff we found."

I dug past my well-worn and half-squeezed out bathing suit and other sand-encrusted laundry to the bottom of the suitcase. Out came zipper bags full of sea shells and plant parts. I opened them up and showed the contents, reciting what things were and what we'd learned about them. As I talked, Rosella took each item and laid them out on the table. When I ran out of things to show, I talked about our cook outs, seining in the warm salt water, fishing, making s'mores, and best of all, swimming. "I probably left a few things out, but I'll think of them later," I said.

Rosella had now heard a few of my stories twice but paid just as much attention as the first time.

When I finally caught my breath, she pointed at the sand around the suitcase. "I can tell you liked the beach. You brought it all back with you. I'll be right back. Keep talking," She strode into the right front room where she kept the washing machine and came back with a laundry basket. "Next time, we'd better send along some plastic bags for your wet laundry."

Next time? My heart jumped up and down and clapped at those words.

I filled the basket with clothes and emptied the sand from the suitcase, banging it upside down to get it all out. Most of it would fall right through the cracks in the cabana floor.

"Open it up, and we'll dry it over here," she said, pointing to a sunny spot.

Eduardo grinned as I dragged it over and kept right on talking. There was so much to say, and more stories from camp were coming back to me now.

"Whew! I have never heard you talk so much, Coral. You certainly had a great time."

By now I was getting winded. "It was the most super time in the whole world. Thank you so much, Rosella and Eduardo. I never thought I'd get to go to camp like that. Even if I never went again, it's the most wonderful thing I ever, ever did." I threw my arms around each of them and squeezed hard.

I never did think to ask what they did while I was gone, though.

There must be a saying somewhere, *The higher the wave, the deeper the trough.* But I was happy to ride that high wave for most of the summer.

Science camp wasn't even out of my system before I wandered down to the stream behind Rosella's one day. Since Mama and I had moved into the park I hadn't really had time to explore it yet, or even found a reason before Rosella and I walked down there, and I'd spotted those vines. The trees were filled with vines. I now had a purpose—to find out whether the vines would hold me—to find out if I could swing across the water on them.

So I strolled down the bank again, nearly sliding into the water as I clambered down the sandy slope. I kept my eyes open, always wary of snakes or alligators. But my main focus was on the fat vines, some of them three inches across, that entwined the trees. I'd like a good Tarzan vine, the real deal. Some hung a little looser than others, but none dangled completely free. Most of them held tight to the tree trunks, a big disappointment. Several loops did hang over the water, so maybe I could borrow a saw and cut one in half.

In the meantime, I clamped onto the best one I could find, and tried swinging. Not much sway and not much fun. Not like a rope. I finally gave up and dropped onto the sand. I needed a real rope.

And that's when I found it. The pebble village.

This creek was someone's playground.

That someone had built a little stone fence row, houses of stacked rocks, sticks, and bark, and had left half-buried miniature trucks along furrowed roads in the bank which has mostly washed away in a rain.

Funny thing was, I'd never seen anyone playing down here. And there were no kids in our park.

Rosella would know less about what went on down at the creek than I did. She never went down there. So I kept the incident to myself and never mentioned it.

Eventually the excitement of camp settled, and I prodded Rosella about my earning the sewing basket.

"I've given that some thought," she said, and sat me down at her kitchen table with milk, a plate of cookies, a pencil, and a notebook.

She snacked along with me for a few minutes. Then a broad smile crept over her face. "I have a little surprise for you." She reached under the table, pulled out a heavy book and a new notebook off the chair next to her and plopped them down in front of me.

"A cookbook?"

"Welcome to your twenty-four cooking projects."

Twenty-four? I flipped through the tabbed pages, imagining how many different kinds of cookies we might be making. But it contained many other things.

"We'll plan six meals with a starch, meat, vegetable, and dessert. Keep track of your recipes in your new notebook."

I nodded. *Not cookies? She wanted meats and vegetables? Real foods? Wow.*

Besides cookies, I didn't know *anything* about cooking other foods.

But I had learned a lot about cookies.

She patted my hand. "Relax. You're not going to do it all at once. Just one dish a day."

My heart sank. Only one a day? Overloading me wasn't the problem. At this rate, it would take forever to earn my sewing basket.

I sat up straight and pulled the notebook toward me. "Could we start today?"

She paused, a curious look passing over her face, and then chuckled. "We could speed things up after a while, but we need to *learn* our cooking skills, not rush through everything."

While she gathered our dishes and tidied the kitchen, I thumbed through the pictures in the book. My mouth watered at all the wonderful cakes, pies, and roasts.

"We'll work out in the cabana where there's more space."

I loved it out there.

My gaze darted around her tiny but spotless kitchen. It certainly beat our own battered kitchen with its hotplate and useless stove. I stuck my nose back into the book.

"There are a couple of catches, though," Rosella said, "so how about you close that for now and listen up."

I nodded and eased it shut, not appreciating the delay. I wanted to get started.

She tapped the notebook tabs. "We'll shop and keep a record of expenses in here."

I nodded.

"This way you'll be ready when you have your own family."

When I have my *own* family? *Me?* Girls my age only dreamed about things like that, but here was Rosella pretty much saying it would happen.

Then there was Mama at my age. She hadn't been ready.

Rosella brought me back to the present. "Most important of all, Eduardo is going to enjoy this as much as we are. He has to okay our choices and grade the results."

I couldn't wait to pass *his* approval.

"And you know, he loves anything Cuban."

I grabbed the pencil from the holder next to the salt and pepper and began my list, part of it straight from my fourteenth birthday party: black beans and rice, fried plantains, yuca, tuna steaks in sauce, mango sherbet, flan, ropa vieja, and Cuban salad. I'd learn it all.

"You'd better save space for some American foods, though. You might not marry a Cuban."

Marry? I couldn't help but grin. The idea that I could have a normal life like Rosella and other families warmed me up inside.

"One big rule," Rosella said. "Some of every dish goes home to your Mama."

That was easy, but I wished she could learn to cook, too, like other mothers.

Chapter 17

Cooking lessons meant I practiced a lot of math. Rosella loved to invite company, and every couple of weeks we invited the Heroes Club into the cabana. That meant doubling the recipes. Fractions all made sense now. I grew very handy with them and with entertaining and planning—Rosella-style.

We gathered ideas from etiquette and decorating books to decorate the tables.

In the beginning, Rosella sent plates of food to Mama in Corelleware dishes and included the silverware. "Just tell your mom to keep them; they're extras," she said.

Good. No more thin paper plates at home.

"Besides," she added, "they'll match your mom's new placemats."

My presentation of the placemats had been forgotten in the shuffle the night of my back-door escape. But Mama eventually got around to thanking us for them and was proud of them. We used them all the time those days.

And now we had plates.

One stormy night, Mama returned from work. I didn't hear her at first.

The racket of battering rain had coaxed me into my bed-roll where I'd fallen fast asleep.

Plip! A drop of water hit my face. I reached to wipe my cheek and *plip!* Another one. I opened my eyes completely.

Above me hovered a Styrofoam container in Mama's outstretched hand.

"Blueberry pie," she said and set it in front of me. She switched on the lamp. Now that she had my attention, she slid onto our plastic covered sofa to kick off her shoes.

"What?" I mumbled.

"Peace offering." She paused for a long beat and watched me rise on my elbows to study its contents, the somewhat dried and most likely expired remnants from today's bakery case. "A mother-to-child gift," she added.

Her feet came off the floor, and she nestled down on the couch until her head lay on the armrest, her eyes close to mine. "I-I just want to say, Coral…" She hesitated as if remembering a rehearsed line. "I'm sorry for it all. I really am."

Even from this distance, I could tell her breath was clear tonight, free from alcohol. Yet I had no clue what she was sorry for.

Her creepy boyfriend? He hadn't returned since the attack.

Another one had, though. And that one in particular scared me to death.

I twisted around backwards to check the front door. No one there.

Not sure how to respond, I waited for more.

"I'm a crummy mother."

I sighed and pressed my hand against hers on the armrest. "Thanks for the pie, for thinking of me, Mama. It's okay. Really."

My lie hung in the air.

I closed the container and set it on the table for tomorrow. But Mama's eyes were already closed. She wore a smile that said my answer was all she needed. I crawled to my knees, flicked off the lamp, and then curled up in my warm nest again.

Being dog-poor was one thing.

But those awful men coming and going and running me out—or touching me—that was another thing altogether.

Being constantly afraid—having to leave my trailer and spend my nights in Rosella's cabana, as nice as it was—that wasn't okay. Not at all.

Why couldn't Mama see that? Why should I even have to explain it to her? The girls at science camp didn't have all those worries.

Mama didn't really care about me.

And like she said, that did make her a crummy mother.

I hated her for it.

But on the other hand, I still loved her. I had to. She was *Mama* after all.

But why did *my* mama have to be this way?

I could not get back to sleep. Instead, I flipped to the left, flipped to the right. Stared at the ceiling. Rosella's image appeared in my thoughts. She hadn't cared about her child, either. Not back then.

And unlike us, she wasn't poor. Far from it.

Truth was, she was no better than Mama. Not back then.

Crummy mother.

I hated those words. I hated the unfair truth of it.

I flipped again, facing the couch. Light filtered in from the streetlamps and spread cold square lines across the back wall, streaked with raindrops, a miserable sight tonight.

Over on the couch Mama purred in her sleep, her face pale, her black apron against her white dress as clear and sharp as daylight to me.

At least she'd considered her ways—figured out she wasn't doing a mother's job. She'd told me as much.

I stared at the stained ceiling. Rosella's image reappeared, her braids, her little pink slippers and gown.

When had *she* come to her senses?

Somewhere along the way, things changed for her. I could swear to it. I knew her. She wasn't a crummy anything anymore.

But her son hated her, and now she was paying the price.

A few feet away, Mama rustled in her sleep. Her hand extended over the edge of the couch, with fingers curled—and innocent.

I imagined Rosella's own small but weathered fingers—how they'd helped me in so many ways.

If Rosella had changed, then Mama could, too.

And I didn't want to treat her bad like Rosella's son had treated *her*. I wanted to be there when she changed.

If only Rosella's son could see *her* now.

Chapter 18

By the next day the storm had passed, and now a wonderful mid-day sun poured into the cabana.

Eduardo's chair butted up to the end of the work table, and before him lay his jewelry-making kit and jewels across a black velvet cloth. An even larger yellow cloth spread underneath it all. I leaned across the table beside him and watched as he dropped a large garnet into a silver Jack-in-the-pulpit mount. Maybe if I paid enough attention, he'd let me try to make something one day.

A few feet away Rosella lounged in one of the softer pillow-chairs reading *Gone with the Wind*, a big fat novel set in the Civil War. "Nothing like a good novel to teach us history," she liked to say.

I fingered one of the larger jewels on Eduardo's velvet. "Are they all real?"

He nodded.

"And valuable." Rosella's gaze strayed from her book to us. "Eduardo has enough gold and jewels locked away to open a jewelry store."

I had no idea.

"That's what he did in Vegas. He designed jewelry. We closed up shop and moved here."

A question had been nagging me ever since I saw those dresses of Rosella's. "Why did you quit show business?"

"Why did I quit?"

I nodded.

She laughed and gazed down at her book. "Cigarettes." She pointed to her throat. "Ruined this."

I had no idea she'd ever smoked. I waited for more, but that's all she said about it. My attention returned to Eduardo and his jewelry making.

"Best thing that ever happened," Rosella said, her eyes back in the book. "Getting out of that town."

I wasn't sure how to reply. I had nothing to add, so I let it drop and once again silence settled over us leaving only the street sounds of slow-moving cars and tiny birds that flitted about and *chip-chip-chipped* up in the trees.

With everything so quiet, I thought this might be the right time to share my little problem. The birds kept up their business as I tried to figure out how to begin.

I cleared my throat. "There's—there's this thing I've been a little— worried about," I said.

Rosella raised her eyebrows and slid a marker in the book. She stuffed it down beside her and turned my way.

Eduardo's tweezers paused in mid-maneuver.

"Is the biker back?" Rosella asked.

I shook my head.

The air tightened. They weren't going to like this. Neither did I. But I didn't know what else to do but bring it up.

"There's—now there's a new guy coming over."

Rosella cleared her throat. "Okaaay." No hint of a smile. "Go on."

Eduardo laid his tweezers on the mat.

I hesitated. "Well, he hasn't come inside the trailer, but I'm afraid he might. He wants to. He keeps staring at me through the doorway. The other night Mama told him to get lost. But he keeps coming back, knocking on the door without having anything important to talk about. Acting like he's trying to talk to Mama but looking in through the door—at me."

Eduardo caught Rosella's eye and nodded. He motioned toward the rear of the cabana.

She returned the nod and stood. "It's time."

Chapter 19

Rosella, not the usual sweet Rosella, but Warrior Woman Rosella rose and strode down the pink boardwalk into the trailer. I raced to catch up and followed as far as the kitchen where she exited the front door. It clicked shut behind her, and I stayed inside. No doubt she was headed over to see Mama.

Whenever they talked, I was not invited. And they never let me in on what was said.

Within seconds, Rosella reappeared. Wordless, she entered the kitchen and yanked open the junk drawer. The scowl on her face and the clamped lips told me how upset I'd made her.

"I'm sorry, Rosella."

Papers and tools rustled left and right as she scrabbled for whatever it was. *Aha.* Out came a large important-looking white envelope that I'd never seen before.

Neither had I seen her like this.

"No, dear," she said as she checked the front of the envelope. "You've done nothing wrong. Nothing at all."

I caught the envelope's Florida logo with its distinct *DCF* lettering as she folded it and tucked it under her arm to head back outside. Once again, the front door slammed.

Quiet hung in the room, all but the faint twittering of birds outside and the steady *tick tick tick* of the clock on the stove. And the echo of the door.

I glanced at the clock. Mama was probably just waking up to go to work.

I spent a long time at the kitchen table. I wanted to be there when Rosella returned. To hear what she had to say.

Finally—her footsteps. The front door opened, and I jumped up.

"Your mom and I had a talk. And we came up with a plan," she said, the envelope still in her possession.

Mama's car engine started up next door. I peered through the curtains and watched her drive away to work.

Rosella touched my shoulder and led me to the sofa. "I know what I have to say might upset you a little, but your mama agrees it's for your protection."

Rosella laid it all out for me. The cabana was to be more than just my get-away place now.

"This will be your new home."

I was to pack up all my things—today—and bring them over to Rosella's.

Live here? With Rosella and Eduardo? In this nice place?

"Do you need help packing?"

I shook my head.

I closed my eyes to process her words. But prickles of bright light and ink rained behind them. Bright speckles of protection—*I was safe now*—falling among black specks of—*what? Guilt?*

My mama would be all alone now.

On my way out her door Rosella handed me a stack of brown paper bags. "Are you sure you don't need help?

I shook my head. This wouldn't take long. And I could do it by myself.

Inside our old trailer I rounded up my things. They filled two grocery bags, and I set them beside the sofa.

For all the selfish times I'd longed for a better situation, I should have felt more joy now, more excitement, more appreciation for my new situation.

But my heart was like a wet sack of wet cement. I crumpled to the floor beside those two wrinkled bags and bawled my eyes out. Rosella couldn't see me like this. Ungrateful and sad.

I wiped my nose on my arm and cried for Mama and how alone she would be. And for how I wanted to be there for her when she changed into a better mama.

I tried to imagine her like that. It helped, and eventually my tears stopped. I dried my burning face and climbed to my feet.

What could I do for Mama? I'd pick her a jar full of those white wildflowers and ferns from down by the stream.

Spanish needles grew all along the banks, and it only took a few minutes. I cleaned out an empty peanut butter jar from the trash and used it for a vase. I filled it with water and placed it on the coffee table next to a single placemat with a plate, a fork, and a knife.

She would love that.

Of course, she'd always be here, right next door.

My voice still choked. "Bye, Mama."

I lifted my bags and closed the door behind me.

Chapter 20

School would start in a few weeks. Nobody could rightfully call me trailer trash anymore. I lived in a fine cabana.

But then, how would they even know?

Rosella sewed and shopped and did everything she could to get me ready. Just like she'd done before camp.

The start of my school year had never been important to anyone before.

What a fuss.

"Oh, you're going to have a great school year," she kept saying.

My heart still ached. Not because I was away from Mama's mess. And not because she wasn't here to enjoy this clean place and the company of Rosella and Eduardo and all their friends.

Mama was still close by. A long invisible cord stretched from my heart to hers over there in her lonely little trailer. We were still connected.

It ached because I left her. Deserted her.

Soon after I moved out, Mama started waking up a little earlier most days and coming to visit Rosella before work.

Maybe she felt the cord, too.

And that lightened my heart. A lot.

She and Rosella seemed to enjoy talking on the front deck while the Heroes Club played cards.

She even laughed.

I don't recall Mama visiting or laughing with anyone before. This was a new side of her, and I liked it.

There were times, though, that Rosella and Mama only talked of adult things, like the Bible. I think they also talked of those men friends of Mama's because sometimes, they would shoo me inside to *read books*. It didn't bother me at all. Mama was nearby.

My heart wasn't sick anymore.

One night, Rosella sat beside me on my pink bedspread. We'd stocked and arranged my desk and bookcase for the upcoming school year with new *everything* and were admiring it all. "Why don't we decorate the room with some of your camp collections?" she said. "We could even frame and label them. Eduardo can help."

I nodded, imagining how that would look.

"While you were at camp," Rosella told me, "I started some classes."

I frowned, not sure what she was talking about.

"I'll take a few more, and then I'm done. I'll be a certified foster parent."

I nodded. What did that mean for me?

"There won't be much of a difference," she said. "But this will be your address, and I can sign your school papers and such. In fact, I'll even take you to school on the first day."

"But Mama will still be my mama, right?"

She pressed her cheek against mine. "Always and forever, Coral."

But within a few more months that comfort would be shaken like an earthquake.

It was a Saturday morning in late October. Our school field trip to Edison's and Ford's Winter Estate was a little more than two weeks away.

"I have to get that permission slip back from Mama," I reminded Rosella. "She hasn't signed it, and it's due Monday.

Mama had come to visit Rosella a lot lately, and for quite a few days they'd been talking about topics so serious I was not allowed to listen in much at all. So I'd put off asking her to sign it. In the meantime, why couldn't she just sign my permission slip and bring it over to Rosella's?

I was looking forward to the big adventure. But, as with all field trips, there was a cost.

"No responsibilities, no money," Rosella would remind me now and then. Sometimes she'd point at my nose and look into my eyes. "I. Will. Not. Spoil. You, Coral. I love you too much." I did not mind that. So as soon as I learned of the field trip, I got right down to business and found out what chores I needed to do to pay my way.

I'm sure part of her own grief was the spoiling of her only son—neglecting him while at the same time giving him everything he wanted. So I kept true to my word and prayed for the Lord to save him and help him live right.

The work she assigned me, though, like the cooking lessons, had been more fun than anything else. I'd long since earned my sewing basket, and it sat top and center of my bookcase beneath the new shadowboxes of rocks, leaves, and shells Eduardo and I had made.

I glanced past the mango tree to Mama's trailer. *Shoot.* Now her car was gone.

Even though Mama had traipsed back and forth over here a lot lately, I hadn't seen her for the last couple of days.

"Go check and see if she left the field trip slip on the table for you," Rosella said.

So I did.

Never mind the permission slip. What I found nearly killed me.

Chapter 21

I cracked open the front door, and a tidal wave of stink rolled out and hit me in the face—a mix of urine and old blood.

What in the world? I craned my neck and squinted into the darkness. There lay Mama on the sofa. I dove across the room.

"Mama!"

I dropped to my knees beside her trembling form.

Her one arm hugged the bodice of her nightgown, and the other lay at her side. Her glazed eyes turned my way.

A whisper escaped her dry cracked lips. "Help me." It was little more than a breath.

"Mama, Mama." I touched her cheek and almost jerked away. Her skin was so cold. "What happened?" I tried to comprehend the dark smears above her ghost-white knees, the dried blood that soaked her gown and formed black stains on the cushion beneath her.

Another silent whisper. "Get..." Her eyes began to close. "Rosel..."

She had to be dying. I backed toward the gaping door, tried to wrap my head around the scene. "I-I'll get her." A giant drum pounded in my ears. I turned. "I-I'll be right back."

I threw myself out the door and tore through the trees to the only person that would know what to do. "Ros*ella*, Ros*ellaaaaaa!*" I'd never screamed like that before—or since.

I flung open Rosella's front door and ran smack into her shocked face. My fingers gripped the door frame. "It's Mama. Call 9-1-1. *Call 9-1-1!*"

She whirled and grabbed the phone receiver off the wall with two hands. "No. No, no, no!" she said as she wedged it between her chin and shoulder and punched in the numbers.

"She's bleeding everywhere," I wailed. "I don't know what's wrong."

Rosella closed her eyes. "Dear Lord."

She stamped her foot. A strong word rolled out of her mouth. It was the nearest she'd ever come to using a cuss word.

"I warned her. I warned her not to do it," she said, as if she knew exactly what had happened.

I stood there at the door breathing hard, in and out, not knowing what to do, and glancing back toward Mama's. "Hurry," I whispered.

Someone answered on the other end—it seemed like forever but it had to have been mere seconds—and then Rosella gave them the information they needed.

And no—she slammed the phone down—she could *not* hold the line.

She fumbled past me with sorrow stretched over her features. "Oh, Coral," she groaned. "I'm so sorry. I can't believe this..."

I followed her down the steps across the yard.

Rosella kept right on talking. Then she repeated that not-so-nice-word. "I even got her some help..."

I had to race to keep up. All of a sudden, Rosella stopped and whirled as if she'd just now recalled I was there. I bumped into her, and we stumbled. "Whoa," she said, and caught me. She wrapped me in her arms. Her body was shaking. Or was it mine?

A siren howled in the distance.

She leaned away and cupped her hands around my face. "Oh, Coral, I am so sorry about this. Please, you don't need to see her in this condition."

But I already had.

"I'll meet the ambulance," she said. "You wait here."

I nodded, and she departed for Mama's yard.

I couldn't wait, though. Or stay back there in Rosella's yard while.... So I followed as far as the bushes between our trailers.

The siren's yowl grew louder as Rosella made her way up the steps and through the gaping doorway. I hadn't even shut my mama's front door.

The insistent wail grew loud. And louder.

I'd gone off and left her front door open—left my Mama

unprotected. I slid down against the mango tree and sobbed into my hands—afraid to follow Rosella, afraid to stay here—and guilty of leaving my Mama like that...

I'm not sure Rosella knew herself what I should be doing right now. She didn't want me to see things, but this was my mama after all.

The wails increased in volume, then faded quickly to a *woop-woop*. They stopped completely as the ambulance swerved into our street. The silent flickering, flashing vehicle emerged through the trees and swung into our yard and rolled to a stop near the door. Two medics with cases leaped out.

Rosella came back outside and stood with her back to me. She crossed her arms and hung her head as she motioned them on in.

They rushed up the steps. Seconds ticked by. Then nothing. A breeze rustled the tops of the palms and the *chip chip chip* of little birds stirred in the bushes around me. The old trailer seemed to have swallowed up the medics. What were they doing in there?

One came outside to the ambulance and fetched a stretcher. He re-entered. Seconds ticked by. The first man backed out.

I stood.

Then the stretcher eased through with Mama's small form on top.

Rosella noticed me then and widened her stance to block my view. As if that would help. She pleaded with me over her shoulder. "Please, Coral, please go back inside. You don't need to see this."

But I'd seen the sheet over Mama's head. I may have been young, but I know what that meant.

I stood there, numb, clinging to the rough bark of the mango tree. I scraped my tears against its hard surface and sobbed, sinking to my knees. "Mama!"

Whump! Whump! Ambulance doors slammed—and moved away, a silent blinking box rocking silently through the trees.

And as quick as that, my mama vanished.

Forever.

Chapter 22

Mama's funeral happened at the Baptist church. Thousands of unfamiliar things led up to it and are still a blur. I never saw so many flowers in my life. The three of us mourned quietly on the front row, with Rosella gripping my hand on one side and Eduardo patting my arm on the other. I sat there with a lump in my throat that I couldn't swallow.

My heroes were all there, my principal, my home-room teacher, and many people I never even saw before.

My camp friends sent sweet cards and flowers, but their mamas didn't bring them to the funeral. Children don't need to think of someone's mama dying. I understood.

A lot of Rosella's friends—and all the heroes brought flowers and food over to Rosella's—our place.

My home now. Forever, I supposed.

With all the company and friends the lump in my throat grew smaller and smaller.

A few days later, Rosella had gathered most of Mama's things and boxed them up.

"You can have them someday when you're ready."

I wasn't. And I wouldn't be for a long long time.

On Saturday men came to hitch up our old trailer and haul it away. Our landlords had called them.

"You don't have to watch," she told me. But I wanted to. I leaned against Rosella beside the mango tree, and we cried together along with Eduardo.

The old trailer, jacked-up now behind the tow-truck, wobbled away. It creaked and groaned. I stared, mesmerized at the empty patch of sand where it once sat and at the cloud of dust that trailed it out to the road—final molecules of what had been.

My tears dripped because of its finality. Within those rickety walls, Mama and the few good things I had learned about her had now departed. They were scooped up and taken away—like a book thrown in the trash—a fearful and sad book that I could never enjoy or handle or look at again.

On the other hand, then neither could those awful men. There was no place for them to go.

I gave Rosella a squeeze and a half smile. "Can we go home now?"

For days Mama's recent habit of visiting Rosella left us with the feeling she might come walking through the trees for another visit.

Oh, I missed her so aching much.

This time it wasn't me who'd left.

It was Mama.

Chapter 23

A few days after the funeral, Rosella went to war.

A praying war. At least that's how I saw it.

Our morning route took us past a corner clump of trees and a small white building in the back of a wooded parking lot. Out by the road a little sign said, *Unwanted Pregnancies.*

"Hold this please," she told Eduardo and shoved her purse into his lap—she wasn't the least bit gentle—and dug out that bottle of anointing oil. I glanced over at Eduardo, but he was busy watching her face.

She motioned for me to follow. "Come on, Coral. I should have done this a long time ago."

She uncapped the anointing oil and held it upside down in her hand with her finger over the opening. Then she set off at a quick pace around that block. Not sure what was going on, and not wanting to be left behind, I bolted to catch up. I followed a few feet behind her. Oily drops fell from Rosella's hand and landed every few feet along the sidewalk. I kept close and tried to make out her quiet prayers. Two things were clear: she definitely didn't like this downtown business with its black and white sign, and she didn't want it to succeed.

At the first corner she stopped abruptly. I smacked into her. She said nothing about it but prayed a little longer there. She also took that opportunity to dab oil on my forehead. "Dear Lord, put Your giant angels of protection around Coral. Make them like those tall palms on McGregor Avenue." Then she marched on.

As I followed, I glanced around searching for the angels. Yet I saw nothing. They must be invisible.

She spoke Chinese or something else. I couldn't tell what, for sure, but a different language came out.

It seemed like an intrusion to listen in on another's prayers, but on the other hand, she'd told me to come.

On the way around the block, she stopped at every corner and prayed extra-long until we reached Eduardo again. Her bottle was now empty. She breathed a big sigh. I commented on the container's empty state. "I'll fill it up again," is all she said. And we strolled on home.

She never mentioned the episode again. But I wanted to. I wanted to know more.

Out in the cabana one day I tried to bring it up, but she simply responded, "When the time is right, we'll talk about it. When the time is right."

Sometimes Rosella didn't talk enough.

I let it drop. For now.

But she added, "Understand this, Coral. I know things about your mom that you don't."

Of course. She knew a whole lot of things I didn't. I wished I knew even a fraction of what she did.

"And your mama's in Heaven."

"How...?"

"I'm certain she is, and I've a story to prove it."

That's when she told me the story of the thief on the cross and his last-minute decision to be on Jesus' side. And he'd ended up that same day in paradise with Jesus.

I wanted to believe Mama was there. In Heaven.

But Mama had no religion.

None.

"Trust me for now. She is."

"How...?"

"I know things."

I wanted to believe it.

"When the time is right. It has to be right. And right now, you're not ready for it."

But I wanted right now to be the right time. And even though when I pressed the point later and it turned out good, I ended up hurting Rosella's feelings.

I let some time pass before I asked about it again. I couldn't help it.

We'd visited the ice cream shop and were on the way back. Rosella had treated me to a cone, a mid-afternoon girls-only break while Eduardo was busy at home working on his jewelry.

A half block ahead loomed the corner with the trees. Beyond them sat the white building with its sign, *Unwanted Pregnancies,* and the sidewalk where Rosella had dripped the oil.

I had to know more about it. "Rosella, don't you think the time is right now?"

She licked her cone in silence as we walked away from the shop. Then as if she'd only just now heard the question, she turned. "What time is right?"

"About this place," I said, as it came into view behind the trees. "And the magic anointing you did," I said.

She nearly choked. "Oh, dear Lord, help us," she said. She stared at me for a long moment. A hurt expression covered her face. "Is that what you thought? After all this time? That it's magic?"

In mid-bite I gaped back at her. I'd never seen her like that and couldn't figure what I'd said wrong.

She stopped under the trees, finished off her cone, and then wiped the napkin across her lips. "I'm sorry, Coral. I'm shocked at myself that I gave you the wrong idea."

I stopped too, scrambling to figure out how I'd messed this up.

I didn't wonder for long.

"When I anointed you, Coral, way back there under the mango trees that night, this oil..." She fumbled through her purse and came out with the precious vial of oil cradled in her palm. Somewhere along the way she'd refilled it. She pressed her other hand across it. "This sacred oil, honey, it's not magic. It represents God's mark. God's claim to something. Not *magic.*"

Okay. I nodded, blinking.

"Symbolic. Not magic." She pressed it against her heart, and then slipped it back into her purse. She shook her head. "I have certainly messed up. God forgive me. I failed to communicate, didn't I? Back at the house I'll give you some Bible verses for it."

She took a few steps, and I realized we were moving on. I licked my cone again, hoping she'd tell me something else.

She shook her head again. "Magic! What an abomination. You need to understand. Magic, spells, potions, witchcraft, they have *nothing, nothing, nothing* to do with your Heavenly Father. Not white magic, not black magic, not purple, cute, funny, or even polka-dotted magic."

If something was wrong with magic, I didn't want anything to do with it. I nodded a little stronger, starting to get it. "I'll read everything," I said. "Just point me to it." I stuffed the bottom end of my cone in my mouth. Rosella knew a whole lot more about things like this than I did. And this must really be important.

I swallowed. "I'm sorry," I said, taking her hand in my somewhat sticky one.

"Oh, Coral. You forgive *me*. This is all my fault for not communicating better. But you talk to the Lord about it. That's what counts." I could still tell she was crushed by my misinterpretation. "Forgive me, Coral, that I didn't make it clear from the start."

I tried to think back to the first time she'd prayed for me. What she had said. "So…" I was treading lightly. "What happened here?" I asked, pointing to the sidewalk.

She tipped her chin about to answer...

But I interrupted. I thought I knew. "You claimed it for God? Put His mark on this place?"

She rallied then and nodded firmly. "Precisely."

I sighed, and we moved on. Just like those angels she'd prayed for God to put around me, I couldn't see how claiming or placing a mark on something would make a difference.

How could it?

On the Monday following Mama's funeral, Rosella walked me into the school office. Her fingers held my permission slip—a black and white copy of it—touched up with Wite-Out. The original, with its bloody prints, she'd left at home.

Rosella had gone back and found it on Mama's living room table. Completely filled out with the money beside it.

I was so proud of Mama.

Rosella set her purse on the high reception desk and waved me toward a chair nearby. "I need to talk to the secretary."

From my low vantage point all I could only see was the other lady's head, her serious face, and the way she kept sneaking looks at me.

I bet not many kids' mothers had died recently. To avoid her attention, I turned my face to the door but still felt her looking at me.

For a school day like today, Rosella and I had arrived fairly early while the office was still quiet. But though I strained my ears, I still couldn't hear more than a word or two of the conversation between Rosella and this lady.

I did catch the words *custody* and *foster parent*, and turned my eyes in time to catch Rosella's finger against her lips. The secretary pursed her own mouth, and that ended their talking and my eavesdropping. In the meantime, Rosella dug in her purse and handed over a few more papers.

Foster-child papers, for sure.

I was an orphan now—with no mother or father.

A kid with papers.

"Thank you, ma'am," Rosella said. "I'll walk Coral down to her teacher if it's okay."

The secretary printed Rosella a visitor's pass. I rose, shouldered my book bag, and we stepped out in the hall. She wrapped an arm around my shoulder and whispered in my ear as she led me away, "Start calling me Grandma from now on, you hear me? I'm gonna be your Grandma Rosella."

I stopped in my tracks. "For real?"

I'd like nothing better than to be her granddaughter.

She nodded.

"Like—adoption?"

"Hmm. Now that's an interesting thought."

My heart lit up. "You could adopt me—as your daughter."

With a half-laugh she gave my nose a tweak. "Oh, honey, that's so sweet, but nobody could replace your mother."

It wasn't meant as a joke. "I didn't mean *replace.*"

We took a few more steps. "Besides, just think..." Rosella grinned and threw her arms wide in exaggerated expression. "Wouldn't that make you Sol's sibling?" She knew I'd heard Sol's mean old nasty voice through the phone when he talked to his mother. "How would you like to be dear Sol's sister? And just think, that would make you my grandson's *aunt.* And he's your age."

Gross! A kid my same age?

I hadn't met his son, but I didn't want to be some kid's aunt. Especially one related to a loudmouth guy like Sol.

Truth was, all I wanted was Rosella.

I jostled her hand back and forth as if to erase her comment, "Come on, Ros...*Grandma,* stop joking around. It's not funny."

But then, I kind-of wish she *would* go ahead and adopt me the mother-child way—without Sol and his kid being in the picture. Besides, even with them—problems and all, at least I'd *have* a family.

Peter Cordero would know what to do.

Things were too complicated.

I thought about her new name. *Grandma.* Rosella would make the perfect grandma. I formed the word with my mouth. It felt good to say it. Hey, maybe she could adopt me as a grandmother. But people don't do grandmother-grandchild adoptions. I hadn't heard of it, anyway.

Our feet *squick-squick-squicked* against the shiny tiles, and Rosella said no more.

It was a long way to the end of the hall and my homeroom. As we passed by each classroom I peeked inside. Not one teacher glanced up. They were too busy preparing for the day, for the herd of children that would soon be here.

I glanced sideways at Rosella. She said nothing more about adopting me. It was clear she didn't like the adoption idea.

Maybe she thought I was ungrateful. Or insulting.

An unease grew in my stomach. I was sorry now that I'd mentioned adoption.

She wanted to be my grandmother, and I shouldn't have asked for more. Now she'd think I was unthankful.

But as an orphan without a mama, it left me floating in the sea like Eduardo's raft—with no place to land. For the first time I sensed how Eduardo and his friends felt with sharks all around.

I was afloat with no kin.

What would happen to me now?

Grandma. At least I had that. And I'd hold on tight. With everything I had.

I'd just forget the adoption thing and be thankful to have a Grandma that loved me. In my very small experience, I knew this was more than most orphans had.

I stopped in the middle of the hall and slid my bag to the floor. I needed to hug her full-on. "I love you, Grandma. Thank you so so much."

"And I love you, sweetheart," she whispered, "with all my heart."

Chapter 24

The end of middle school brought the announcement of a prom. High school was just around the corner, and we were going to celebrate in the gymnasium with a live-band dance, decorations, and a refreshment table.

I burst into the trailer. "Grandma! Grandpa!" It wasn't long before the habit of calling them Grandma and Grandpa took hold. Sometimes I stretched it out and called her Grandma Rosella, or him Grandpa Eduardo.

No response.

I un-shouldered my book bag. "Grandma! Grandpa!" Still no answer. They must be out back. I hooked it over my arm and raced down the boardwalk to find Rosella sewing in the cabana. Eduardo, with Yap Yap on his lap, worked nearby on his jewelry.

He glanced up and grinned at me. I kissed them both and dropped the heavy satchel on the floor.

"You're not going to believe this," I said, perching on a chair between them. I was ready to burst. "Three different boys asked me to the prom. Three!" I held up the fingers to make my point.

Things had certainly changed for me since that day at the ice cream shop.

Switching schools this year had also helped, thanks to dear Rosella, and now I had lots of friends. It was her idea to request a more academic school. Parents don't get to choose their child's school, and I don't know what strings she pulled, but it happened. To me, she was the most wonderful person in the world, along with Eduardo, of course, and the best thing that had ever happened to me.

Whatever it was that made Rosella the way she was, I wanted to be just like her.

Eduardo—who adored me calling him Grandpa—nodded in a satisfied way and raised a high five for me to slap. It was his way of saying congratulations. I rose, slapped his hand, and traded hugs with him.

I curtsied. "Thank you very much, Grandpa."

He pointed to his jewelry mat and tools and with those wonderful expressive hands of his indicated that he was going to make me something special.

"Oooh! I can't wait to see what you come up with!" I gave him an extra kiss on the cheek.

Rosella now stood beside me with her palms pressed together. Her face glowed. "That's wonderful. We need to design you a dress."

I'd grown to love her fashions and bold artistic liberties. We'd collaborated on quite a few things, and I'd created outfits on paper, and for Barbie dolls—which I owned plenty of now, but did *not* play with—and some for myself.

My closet was running over with clothes, unlike before when I didn't even need a closet.

It's not that I needed that kind of wardrobe. Grandma wasn't trying to spoil me. But she did love to sew. And I certainly earned the cost of the fabrics by working around the house. My contentedness didn't come from the garments. I might even feel guilty with so many.

But the fact is, clothes were just so much *fun* to make.

I loved designing, and now spent a lot of spare time doodling and thinking up new things. Even at church, as bad as it sounds, I'd catch myself studying peoples' clothes around me and how they were put together.

And all the time in the back of my mind I kept wondering what special thing I could create for Rosella.

"We'll start whenever you're ready," she said. And I could tell she was chomping at the bit to collaborate on that prom dress.

I held up my finger. "What if I come up with something this time?"

She pressed a hand against her heart. "Oh, yes. You think it up, and I'll make it. Whatever you like."

I squealed and unzipped my back pack to find some paper. "I've got just the idea."

It was late Friday evening. Supper dishes were put away and the three of us were out in the cabana as usual. Rosella had reached the final two chapters of her latest Frank Peretti book, and wanted to finish it before bedtime.

Eduardo motioned me over to his jewelry-making spot, wanting to include me in his necklace design to match my prom gown. He had a rough sketch of its basic shape and had written me a short note. He hated writing notes. Why he would resist the one easiest way he could communicate, I could not understand. I loved to write.

I read the note. *What kind of blossom do you want?*

Tomorrow he'd create a wax mold for the necklace, and I planned to watch.

He indicated the chair beside him and handed me a book of flowers so I could sit and choose my favorite.

"They're *all* beautiful."

He shrugged as if to say, *Of course they're beautiful,* then dragged his fingertips across the page as if insisting, *but which one?*

I flipped through and shut the magazine. "Roses," I said. "In honor of Grandma Rosella."

One final look to verify, *Are you sure?*

"That's the one," I said.

With a wink he pulled the book away and took up his pencil. He was back at work.

I'm pretty sure he loved my choice. There's nothing prettier than a rose.

I moved over to the chair next to Rosella and fished out my sketch book of designs.

"I think I know what I want," I said, displaying the picture I'd been working on for the past week. It had a lot of erasures, but I'd darkened up the main lines—a sleeveless bodice with an empire waist, and a ruffle that stood up behind the neck and tapered off at the bottom of the v-neck.

"Stunning, Coral. I love it," she said. "In pink?"

I shook my head. My closet held plenty of pink. This might be a good opportunity to try a new color.

"Chiffon? Satin?"

I felt proud to be able to converse with her about the different fabrics. She'd made a point of teaching them to me. "Brocade, I think, something with body."

She tapped her chin and contemplated with a thoughtful expression. "Something that goes with silver, which he plans to use," she said, nodding in Grandpa's direction. "Why don't we go shopping tomorrow?"

I faux-clapped. "I thought you'd never ask."

Her gaze returned to her book. "By the way, which young man did you choose?"

"Well, they're all nice."

A chuckle. "That's good. But remember, it's not fair to keep them hanging on."

I peeked sideways at her. "I wonder who's the cutest."

I'd upset her earlier in the school year when I mentioned having a crush on a guy. The crush wasn't the problem.

"What's he like?" she said.

"He's cute," was the only thing I could come up with.

Her mouth fell open. "No other qualities? That's it? Cute? Nothing more?"

I nodded, trying to figure out real quick why cute wasn't good enough.

"Oh, honey, that's nice, but a relationship is more than just looks. It's about friendship and character first. Looks aren't bad, but good looks, honey, by themselves? They will trip. You. Up. Please, I never want you to fall for somebody's looks."

I frowned, trying to comprehend. "*Cute, cute, cute,* that's the main thing girls talk about at school."

"Well, don't ever let me hear *you* talk like that. The world is full of beautiful people with rotten cores." She crossed her arms. "And I've seen many. They're like a wad of poo poo in a golden package."

She sank her eyes back into her book. After a few minutes she mumbled, "That wasn't too funny, Coral." She knew I was joking about picking the cutest boy for the prom.

"Got yer goat," I said with a grin.

She pointed at me. "Ha, ha, young lady. But my advice stands."

"Yes, pretty is as pretty does, and there are lots of handsome, rotten men. *And* women."

She nodded. "Good. You've listened well. Don't forget it." She paused. "So, on a lighter note, who will it be?"

I groaned in dramatic fashion. "Oh, I don't knowwwww! Maybe I should draw straws."

She dismissed my nonsense with a wave of her hand. "Poor little thing. Only three to choose from. Let me know when you make up your mind." And she went back to her reading.

No more was said as I returned to my notebook and traced a fresh drawing from the old one. I really didn't know which guy to pick. All three were good friends. None were boyfriend types. I didn't need one of those.

By the time Grandma spoke again I'd moved on to other thoughts.

"Character. Pick by character. And friendship."

"Easy for you to say. I wish I could."

"Whatever do you mean?"

"Grandpa. There's no one as good as him, no one. And nobody as handsome."

A knowing look crept across her face as she studied me. The sparkle in her eyes hinted at some mysterious secret.

"What?" I demanded.

"Hmmm," was all she would say.

And no amount of cajoling could get her to say anything more.

Chapter 25

Grandpa Eduardo allowed me to watch as he began forming the wax mold of my necklace. He cut petals and leaves, formed, connected, and shaped. But the clusters of tiny roses would take days. He worked and worked while I was at school, and by the end of the week he and Rosella took the completed pieces out to a local man to be cast in silver. Within a week they come back as solid pieces of metal to be connected with loops and chains.

At this point he refused to let me see it.

One evening I tried to persuade him. Just one little look was all I needed. Grandma intercepted. "Nope, no peeking," she said, taking me by the arm. "But are you ready to see my progress on your dress?"

Her sole focus that week was on finishing the aqua gown. The short time between the prom's announcement and actual event had nearly evaporated.

I nodded. "Of *course!*"

"Well, cover your eyes!" she said and guided me toward my room. Finally, she stopped, opened the door, and pulled my hands away. One glimpse and I squealed. "Oh, Grandma, I love it!" It was beautiful.

There on my dress form, an investment made a while back by her so she could "try things on me" while I was at school, hung our aqua masterpiece, fit for a princess.

"Try it on and don't forget your new silver heels."

My first ever. How could I forget them?

Grandma couldn't stop smiling. She unzipped the gown, slid it off the form and laid it across my bed. "I'll step out the door. You try it on."

I slipped everything on as well as the long matching gloves. At the mirror I pulled up my hair and stared at my grinning reflection.

I wasn't the same Coral anymore, at least not the same twelve-year-old Grandma had found under the mango trees.

Thanks to Rosella and Eduardo, here was the Coral that someone loved and cared about.

And if I was to believe this mirror, almost grown. Here was the other Coral—clean, well dressed, making good grades in school—with talk of going away to college in South Carolina in a few years. I couldn't even imagine it.

Oh, Grandma. And Grandpa. How I loved them.

I stepped through the door and out into the cabana.

Grandma gasped and took a step back with her hand over her heart. "Look how it brings out your eyes!"

Eduardo nodded, blinking slowly in silent approval. He scribbled a note on a scrap of paper. *You're a lovely Caribbean shore.*

I hugged his neck. "Grandpa you are such a poet."

Grandma came close and fluffed out the gathers of my skirt. "Look at you. Just look at you."

Eduardo motioned for me to step over and extended a turquoise box with a silver bow.

The jewelry?

I knelt beside his chair to open it.

"Oh!" I lifted out the most beautiful chandelier necklace in the world. Silver swags and dangles draped from clusters of tiny roses. I pressed the back of his hand against my cheek and then kissed it. "It's perfect, Grandpa. Beautiful. But especially because you made it. I don't have enough words to say how lovely this is. Thank you."

Grandma took the necklace. "Stand up and let me put this masterpiece on you." She fastened it around my neck, and I stood back to model it.

If ever I had doubts about being a foster child, I had no more. Grandma and Grandpa were family, whether they actually adopted me or not. I loved them so much.

But looking back, that sweet world was about to change.

Chapter 26

For the prom, I picked my good friend Jimmy—the one who had partnered with me for the science fair and led us to victory with a second-place ribbon. He claimed it was my doing, and I said it was him. We'd both worked hard and made a great team.

We danced ourselves silly at the middle-school prom and wore ourselves out. Once I slipped a little in my silver heels. Jimmy was right there and caught me by the elbow. I laughed at my clumsiness. But he didn't. Not until he was sure I was okay. And then he smiled.

Over at the punch table, someone bumped his elbow and the punch in his cup shot straight up and doused his arm on the way down. Students stepped away, but a teacher on duty raced toward us with a mop and paper towels. The bumper-guy was truly apologetic. But Jimmy grinned and waved it off. We sopped up the mess, amazed at the size and scope of that red spot—on him and the floor—but Jimmy was unbothered.

What an amazing character. An incident like that could have ruined his night. But it hardly fazed him.

"This will make for good pictures later," he said. Nothing riled Jimmy. Later, he took me by the shoulders and with a twinkle in his eye and as much seriousness as he could muster, said, "I'll never forget you, dear Coral, or this…this…" he could hold it in no longer and burst out laughing, "red science experiment I've become!"

I laughed then, too, sorry for his discomfort, but grateful not to have gotten drenched myself. We dabbed at him with a handful of napkins, and then kept right on dancing. "Aren't you cold in this air conditioning?" I asked.

"Nah," he said, "just getting warmed up now." After that we giggled and snorted about every other silly thing that happened.

I think we enjoyed the prom more than anyone else there. We weren't boyfriend and girlfriend like a lot of kids, just good buddies. After the dance, his parents, a jolly, hefty pair—Jimmy resembled them so much—took us out for photos—some with and some without the red spot showing—and a fondue dinner at The Melting Pot.

It was quite late when his parents brought me home.

Back inside with Grandma and Grandpa Eduardo I couldn't stop talking. My middle school prom was the best ever with so much to tell. I did eventually wind down, totally exhausted, and went off to bed. They were probably relieved.

Within a few days the end of eighth grade arrived. These last three years had been the worst and best years of my life. I passed with flying colors and several awards, one in science, thanks to Jimmy, and the other in art. I was now a high school freshman.

In *high school!*

I tucked away my awards, but Eduardo got Grandma to sneak the certificates back out so he could frame them for the living room wall and show them to all his friends.

And then, for several slow lazy days, I cuddled between the sheets until at least eight o'clock, and nobody disturbed me. Grandma said I had earned it.

But then came June 1st.

Chapter 27

My mattress jostled as Grandma perched beside me. I tried to hold on to my dream, to stay asleep. This was summer, after all.

She jiggled my arm. "Coral, Coral," Her voice was choked, all wrong for her.

I detached from my slumber and peeked out from under my covers. Grandma was dressed in her nightgown. She wiped the back of her hand across her swollen eyes. She'd been crying.

I sprang upright, my heart racing.

"W-what's the matter?"

Rosella was like the birds in the trees, always happy in the mornings. She pressed a sodden handkerchief to her nose. Tears filled her eyes.

"Eduardo's gone."

No. A frigid wave dropped over me... I opened my mouth, but words failed me. I tried again. "Gone?"

Her fingers, with their tissue thin skin, trembled around the wadded fabric. I fixed my eyes on them, avoiding her gaze.

Rosella couldn't mean *gone.*

Not that kind of gone.

Not our Eduardo.

She rose. Reached for my hand. Her voice cracked. "Come."

Somewhere deep inside, that cold wave turned to fiery acid. I climbed out, a wooden marionette, and took Grandma Rosella's hand. We stepped along the endless boardwalk, through the open back door, and all the way to their tiny bedroom behind the kitchen.

Only then did she let go of my hand. She entered first. There was hardly room for her in there, let alone me. I squeezed in behind her.

"I loved him so much," she keened, her voice pitched high like a child's. She touched her fingers to his chest as if to relay the brokenness of her heart.

My own was a hot brick. A brick of acid.

Eduardo, all six feet two of him, lay under the neatly turned-back sheet—a handsome prince. I'd never seen him stretched out like that. Grandma must have fixed him up. Surely, he didn't sleep so neat and tidy.

I stared at his chest, hoping it would move. Hoping Grandma was wrong.

"He went in his sleep," she whispered, her voice hoarse. "The way he wanted it."

Gone. A familiar knot formed in my throat, and I thought of Mama on that bloody couch.

I struggled for a balance, for it to all sink in. Eduardo couldn't be dead. Not my grandpa. He'd just gotten started in my life. *We'd* just gotten started.

I watched his chest. Surely, he would wake up—would breathe. *Wake up, Grandpa.*

I studied his face.

Smile, wink—do like yesterday, move. Anything.

I leaned forward. "Grandpa. Grandpa..." I whispered. Electricity buzzed between my ears.

Rosella moved her fingers to her lips.

Grandpa's hand lay over his chest—had it clutched at his heart? I rested my own hand over it—his was so cold—and then my other. I held them there—cupped, as if they might warm him up and bring him back to life.

Seconds ticked by as the arcs continued their humming inside my brain.

But it was no use. His fingers remained cool, like a sidewalk in the winter when no amount of sitting would warm it up.

Grandpa.

But there he remained. Still. A quiet prince.

He'd slipped away. Just like that.

I could not understand how yesterday he was here—and now he was not.

Rosella's face puckered. My own tears rose. Burned behind my lids. We turned and clutched each other. I sobbed, and so did she. We squeezed hard as if we could press away the ache.

I pictured him as he was the day before. *You were my hero. I love you so much.*

I glanced one more time at his mouth, his closed eyes. They seemed so able, so nearly alive.

And yet they weren't.

And now I closed my own. "Five more minutes," I moaned. "Just five minutes with him, Grandma. That's all I want…"

She nodded against my cheek.

And we stayed that way a good long time.

Chapter 28

After his funeral under the mango trees, which of course ran over into the street because of his many friends, a limousine took Eduardo to be buried in the shade of the moss-covered oaks at Ft. Myers Cemetery.

A newspaper article told of him being a hero.

Afterward, Rosella and I were offered many rides home that day, but we walked back home together. Nothing ever felt so strange as to walk along with Rosella that day without a wheelchair in front of us. That, by itself, was as painful as losing Eduardo all over again. I wondered if we would still take our morning walks now.

But we did. Rosella tried to keep everything the same. She even insisted the heroes come over to play games every day as they used to do. She did it as much for them as for us. She baked her cookies, and the friends came. Just like always.

I was so thankful.

Eduardo's wheelchair remained beside Rosella's recliner in the living room, another thing she kept the same. I half-expected her to wheel it out to the table in the front yard every day, but that would have been weird. Rosella was sentimental, not weird.

Poor Yap Yap spent his days wandering in and out of rooms whining for his owner. He'd plop down beside Eduardo's bed or the wheelchair now, with his head on his paws and blink his big brown eyes.

Since Grandpa Eduardo's death, I hadn't even thought about summer science camp. It was due to start in another week.

After the science camp, Grandma's Baptist church would be sponsoring a sewing camp. The Baptists belonged to me too, I guess, but though I'd been baptized I'd never actually joined the church. I believed like Grandma. And her faith extended a little further than what the church traditionally taught.

She wouldn't talk about the differences with me, and when I asked about it, all she said was, "We have our few differences, but I dearly love my Baptist family."

I knew when the subject was closed.

"You'll figure it out. Search the Bible and think on things like unity, love, and tolerance."

So I decided I would and let it go.

"I can't go to camp and leave you alone," I told Grandma.

"Oh, posh. You're all signed up. And I have plenty of company. I'll not have you give up camp and stay home on my account."

That settled that.

The day before I left for camp, Grandma was out in the cabana reading *The Yearling*—another fat book. I wanted to do some last-minute vacuuming to leave her in good shape and dug out the vacuum cleaner. I rolled it down the boardwalk to her trailer, enjoying the sound as it thumped and bumped like a wagon over a rocky road.

Vacuuming the tiny trailer was no job at all, and I started with the living room, then crossed through the kitchen. Grandma's bedroom door was shut, and I paused there with my hand on the knob recalling the last time I'd been in there—the morning Eduardo died.

He wasn't in there now, I told myself—and gave the door a push.

I squinted. The sun, like the other day, blazed down through that tiny window and lit up the room.

I caressed the bed where Eduardo's body had lain just days ago. It seemed unfair for me to be running off to camp and going on with my life so soon.

But I knew Grandpa would have insisted.

I imagined him smiling and shooing me away to camp. I couldn't help but grin. Never would I wallow in self-imposed bad feelings.

Once again, I flipped on the vacuum. I shut the door again so I could run the vacuum between the bed and the wall.

And that's when I found Rosella's packed suitcase.

<h1 style="text-align:center">Chapter 29</h1>

Grandmaaa!" I burst out of the trailer and raced for the cabana. My feet flew over the boards, and I stopped, bawling, in front of her. It was no use to pretend I hadn't seen the suitcase. I wasn't snooping. Had Eduardo's death hit her so hard that she would desert me? Sneak away while I was at camp?

She dropped her book and stood. "Coral, what's wrong?"

Was I going to lose her too? She couldn't do this to me.

"Where were you going?" I wailed, my arms limp at my sides. "Where?"

"Oh, honey." She wrapped me tight. "I'm so sorry. I didn't want to worry you."

"Where, Grandma, where were you going?" I gasped for air, still confused.

"I'm flying out to see my son and grandson."

I stepped back, rubbing an arm under my nose. "For how long?" I wasn't trusting this. She might not come back.

She pulled me to her shoulder again and patted my head as I heaved and wept against it—my loudest and biggest cry since either funeral.

"I'll be here to pick you up, Coral. I'll be right here."

I wiped my nose again.

"I'd never leave you."

"I-I—okay..." I sputtered. "As-as long as you come back."

Only then did it hit me—her son hadn't even come home to his dad's funeral.

Chapter 30

My mother's nomadic life had loused me up in elementary school and cost me a whole year. Thanks to Grandma's farsightedness, over the span of a few summers, in addition to two weeks of camp, I added in a few summer school courses including drivers' education. "That way you can use the Mustang when you need it—or if I get in a pickle and need your help getting around."

"Stop it, Grandma. Don't talk like that. Just—keep walking, eat healthy, and stay well, okay?"

Using her Mustang was a great incentive. But I especially appreciated her coming up with the summer school idea. "I never would have thought I could make up that lost time. Now I can graduate with my age group," I told her.

The end of my sophomore year drew near, and I'd just celebrated my sixteenth birthday the night before.

Among the party guests were twelve of my best high school friends. Peter came as he always did with a big bakery cake decorated with pink roses and fancy writing. On this occasion it was *Happy Sweet Sixteen, Coral.*

The heroes came too. They wouldn't dream of not being here for me or Grandma. And so far, they were all well, and blessed, and had good sharp minds.

Rosella and I had shoved all the furniture aside and created a large space in the cabana. From the kitchen we served crackers with *queso blanco* and guava paste, dishes of fresh mango from our trees, plantain-wrapped crab cakes, yuca fries with cilantro mayonnaise, roast pork with plantains, and Grandma's famous *tres leches cake.*

The cabana rocked and vibrated with Cuban music and dancing. My heroes, enchanted with my high school friends, took it upon themselves to train them all in the fine points of salsa, *cumbia,* a dance from Colombia, and cha cha cha. My friends loved the lessons and music, and I was sure they'd never look at dancing the same again.

The next morning Rosella and I tidied up the deck and dragged all the furniture back in place. It was a great dance floor.

We were still touching up the kitchen. "Now that you're sixteen, what would you like to do with your life?" Grandma asked as she wiped down the countertop. "What makes you happiest? It's time we get some traction on your plans for college." She turned slightly. "And you *will* be going."

Something about her expecting this of me brought it into reality.

I polished up a glass and placed it in the cupboard. "Grandma, college costs…"

"Nothing at all." Rosella said, pointing a finger at me. "It's taken care of."

"Oh." She'd never mentioned that before. Warm honey poured over my heart.

"Coral, we've always talked of college, and yet I know you can't read my mind. I'm sorry that I haven't verbalized my intentions before. But I don't want you worrying about how to pay for it."

I grinned. "Hey, you said you weren't going to spoil me."

She wasn't to be distracted. "Honey, you know I won't be around forever. And you'll need college in order to take care of yourself. I can't take my money with me. I'd rather help you get started."

I shuddered. "Please don't talk about dying, Grandma. Can't we put this conversation off?"

She guided me by the elbow to our favorite chairs, sat me down, and then pulled her chair around in front of me.

"Let's lay it all out," she said, taking a seat. We now sat face to face. "This place," she waved an arm above her head, "will always be yours. This house, this property. Yours. No matter what happens to me, you'll always have a place to live."

I wrapped my elbows around my knees and looked up at her. "I appreciate everything, so much, and I thank you from the bottom of my heart. But can we avoid mentioning things *happening* to you?"

"Fine. So back to the topic of college, what career would make you happiest?"

My mind drew a blank. Up to this day, college had seemed a goal too far out of my reach. I half-chuckled. "Well, I love to read. But I guess there's no career in reading."

She ignored the joke.

"But I do love designing clothes and writing stories."

"Of course, you do. And somewhere out there, there's a career for both of those. You should follow your heart and go for it. Add in a few business courses for good measure, and study what you like. Get your AA and a good foundation at the community college. Then we'll find you a school for whatever you want. And that's not to say you won't discover a fork in the road along the way and choose something different. But it's a starting point. Right?"

Hearing this concrete plan of action did seem to help. I could now afford to go. And I had a direction, something I hadn't felt the need for before.

How my life had changed—since that night when I was twelve.

"But let's change the subject to something a little more fun. I want to tell you about this." She waved her hand in the air again. "Your home. First, like I said, you'll always have a place to live." She dipped her head and then looked up at me. "But that's not quite the whole story." She paused. "Last week," she said, dragging it out, "Peter and I drew up the papers to put this property in your name when you come of age."

My mouth gaped. "Property? In my name?" I couldn't even wrap my head around that.

"It's not just a place for you to stay, Coral. It's yours now. Happy birthday, sweetie. I thought I'd wait until after the party to tell you. It's not something you want to broadcast."

"Oh, Grandma...!" I grabbed her hands. The way things were going she might as well have adopted me.

"Ready for another sweet-sixteen surprise?"

I gaped at her. The first news was enough, and I hadn't even digested it yet. "I don't think I can handle anything else, Grandma."

She did not pause. "As soon as school's out, you've got a job."

All this news was making me dizzy. I leaned forward. "Wha…?"

She squeezed my hands and grinned. "Peter's office." I'm sure my own expression was one of shock. "We look out for our family around here."

They certainly did. I squealed and jumped up. "Oh, my goodness!" This day was surreal. I wanted to dance. To scream. To pass out on the floor. "No, way, no way!"

Grandma just kept on smiling. "No wild spending. Put your tithe in the offering plate at church and sock the rest of the money away. Then buy a car," she said. "Peter will help you. You're going to need one." I wondered why she didn't offer the black Mustang in the shed.

She seemed to read my mind. "Sit back down."

I did.

"Eduardo has promised the car to Mateo, our grandson. He's giving him all his jewelry, and jewelry-making tools. In the meantime, while you're saving, you're free to use the Mustang."

Mateo. She'd finally given her grandson a name. "It doesn't sound like Mateo's getting much, does it? Compared to me, I mean."

"We're not comparing, but are you kidding? Eduardo left enough in that safe deposit box to open a jewelry store. That was Eduardo's trade back in Vegas, remember? He designed custom jewelry."

I raised my eyebrows. It was all news to me. How did Rosella continue to come up with so many surprises?

"What about your son? Does he get something, or does he get left out?"

Since she brought it up, I figured I might as well ask.

"Don't you worry. He'll get just what he wants. Cold green money."

"I've been praying for him like you asked. Every day."

"I know you have—you're a dear. I'm praying too. And God is listening. We don't see results yet, but we don't walk by what we see. We walk by faith. And the Good Book says it's God's will that all be saved. If we ask according to His will, it will be done. We just don't know when it will happen."

I held up one hand. "Wait, wait, wait, Grandma. Back to the

property—I thought you were renting this place. How can you give it to me?"

She swatted at an imaginary fly. "I used to rent. But now the park's mine. I'm the landlord."

"You—*bought* it."

She scrutinized my face as I digested the fact.

I gasped. "When? When did you buy it?" That truck the landlord had sent to haul away Mama's trailer—smack on the heels of her death as if getting rid of her memory couldn't wait—had that landlord been Rosella? I couldn't imagine her being so insensitive. Even though that trailer had been a nasty old rat trap.

She touched a finger to her chin and gave it some thought. "Let's see. Maybe a month before Eduardo passed. About the time of your prom that year."

I let out a slow breath. *Good. It wasn't Rosella then.* Mama had died in October.

"About Mama—once we moved into this park, we quit moving around every few months and stayed put for the first time ever. Did you—was that your doing?"

"We didn't own the park then, but we were glad to help her out, and her cute little gal young 'un."

And then it hit me. Grandma owned the entire park, not just her lot. "What exactly are you putting in my name?"

"The whole thing."

I gasped. Here I was, barely sixteen, and I would own a whole trailer park. "Oh, Grandma," I dropped to my knees beside her chair and took her hand. "What can I say? I love you so much. But please, don't use this as an excuse to let something happen to you. Don't go leaving me."

She pulled me to her. "Hush, now." She rocked me back and forth. "I'm right here. And I'll stay as loooong as I can."

Chapter 31

My last two years of high school passed quickly. I graduated with high honors like most of my friends, many of them also summer camp buddies. Thankfully, nothing about those four years of high school carried the same bitter taste as my early middle school experiences.

With the money I earned at Peter's office, he'd helped me pick out a fairly nice refurbished Mustang, a red one close in age to Eduardo's. "Get this vehicle up to school," he said, "but don't try to drive home. Fly home when you need to come. There are plenty of cars here. And don't worry about the air fare. We'll get you home." He certainly spoke for Grandma, but I'd long since learned he was as much a father to me as she was a grandmother. And this advice came straight from his heart.

I thanked him for all he'd taught me at the law office. "I might even change my major," I told him. But we both laughed. He knew I was the artist type, not the confrontational type. Where he reigned tough and cool in court, I'd crumble to pieces. That's okay. As Grandma always said, the world needs all types.

Yet one sad moment did follow my high school graduation.

After the ceremony, my group of friends and their parents filled a grand central table down at the Melting Pot. Fondue had always been our group's go-to method of celebration. We lingered long and loud, making merry and chattering on and on about our upcoming plans for college. Every one of my friends would be going.

As for me and a few other friends, we'd already enrolled at the nearby Keiser University. I planned to stick close to Grandma for as long as possible.

As she and I drove home after the party, we passed the old ice cream parlor. I craned my neck, half expecting to see those two ill-mannered girls sitting on the bench out front. They weren't there, of course. I hadn't seen them in a long, long time. The sun was setting and the shop's neon lights glowed pink, blue, and green:

OPEN
ICE CREAM CONES
MILKSHAKES
HOT FUDGE
SUNDAES
BANANA SPLITS

Since that day long ago, I've preferred other ice cream shops over this one. No matter how pretty their parlor was, or how many times I've visited, this shop always carried with it the sting of the girls' rejection. I'd never met them or learned their names, but I wondered aloud what had become of them.

"Well, God forgive them," I said, returning my attention to the street.

"It sure took me a long time to get over them," Grandma said. "But they did you a service that day."

I stared at her, aghast. "A *service?* It was horrible, Grandma. Painful."

"Well, in a roundabout way they did. But don't you think it started something good for you and me?"

I glanced back at her as we passed a stretch of sunset. For a split second it backlit her cheeks, and once again that circle of braids turned her into an angel.

I shook my head. Grandma always tried to see a silver lining.

"You had me pegged way before that," I said. "But you did have a way with Mama," I added, thinking back to the clever ways Rosella had worked around Mama's insecurities. Grandma could have been a psychiatrist.

"Your mama would have been so proud to see you at your graduation."

"I wish she could have been here," I said, unable to control the catch in my voice. "If...if she'd stayed around—I just know she'd have turned out all right." I turned to meet her gaze. "Don't you think so?"

She closed her eyes to meditate on the question.

"Don't you?" I repeated, slowing the car. The street was nearly empty. "Don't you feel she'd have turned out all right? And become a good person?"

She nodded. "I know she would have."

Without thinking, I turned on the blinker and eased the car into a U-turn. I had to see the place, bring this thing to closure. Not two blocks away on another quiet side street stood that *Unwanted Pregnancies* sign on that peeling whitewashed building. We approached, coasting past a corner clump of trees, our tires crunching over tiny gravel. I rolled down my window and pulled into a parallel parking place across the street. There it sat—the odious place Grandma had anointed.

"Go. Let's not stay here," Grandma said, shifting in her seat. "This is a bad place."

I put the car in park and turned off the engine. I faced Rosella. She'd avoided my questions about why Mama died. Never explained it. All she told me was Mama bled to death. Which she had. And though I suspected the cause, I'd never had the courage to ask her outright. I was now eighteen and grownup enough to handle it. Even if it was as awful as I feared.

"It was an abortion, wasn't it?" I waited a long moment for her answer as humid air drifted in. In the distance children played and a lawnmower sputtered to life then petered out again just as quickly.

I didn't give up. I needed answers. "Isn't that what killed her?"

Rosella closed her eyes and nodded.

We sat in the quiet save for the occasional passing car or an owl who'd begun his *whoo whoo whooing* up in the trees. But there was nothing poetic about our setting. Not with that wicked place beside us.

"She took away my baby brother," I whispered. "Or baby sister. She stole them from me. Stole them."

"She thought she was protecting you."

I snorted. "Protecting me." My voice rose. "You're not defending her, are you?"

She crossed her arms and turned away. "That's not fair. You know me better than that."

"Explain it to me, Grandma. What you've told me doesn't even compute."

"She was trying to protect you. Truly. And one day, though we both disagree one hundred percent with her decision, you'll understand."

"I love her, but I'm still angry with her." I squeezed the wheel with both hands. "And I'm constantly trying to fight off those feelings. If she'd lived, she would have done better. I saw her talking to you in the front yard. Day after day I saw her changing. But I have all these mixed-up feelings, and this story doesn't make sense."

"And I'm telling you she was trying to protect you. In her own wrong way. And she made a mistake. She realized it at the end. She made one desperate move to protect you. Believe, me, sweetheart. You were in danger. And she did love you."

I pressed my fingers against my squinted eyes and then started the motor.

"Let's get away from here," I said. I pressed the gas, spinning grit from under the wheels. I doubted whether I'd ever understand.

Chapter 32

The next two years passed like days. And here we were again, making merry again at the Melting Pot and celebrating the earning of our AA and AS degrees.

Though joyful with our accomplishments, we lamented the fact that half our original group was absent, far away in other states, and that our arrangement of tables and chairs was a severely whittled-down version of our former one.

Within days, the friends now celebrating with me over fondue would leave town. They would disperse even farther—to distant universities. And I'd go on to Charleston to study fashion design and creative writing. Though we still kept up with our out-of-state-friends like Jimmy by social media and texts, we knew that without a clear effort, we'd eventually lose track of each other.

So just like Grandpa's heroes had done, we gave our word to keep ourselves on each others' radars.

I suggested, and everyone agreed, that if we ever needed to find each other we could always go through Peter.

He would be our go-between.

Peter, dear Peter. He was always there.

And now that I was officially an adult, at least in my own mind, I felt comfortable addressing my former boss as "Pete."

Later that evening after our celebration, Grandma and I sat in the cabana, me with a pen and paper making my packing list for Charleston Galena University, and she with a book. I doubted she'd actually read anything, though, as she hadn't turned a page in a while.

She finally spoke up. "Coral, I'm so proud of you. Eduardo and your mama, they'd be proud as punch too if they could see how beautiful and grown up you are."

"Please, Grandma, you're making me sad with all this sentimental stuff."

I was depressed enough by myself, because of leaving Grandma and all my friends and going off to a strange place. Dragging Eduardo and Mama into the mix was overkill.

I scribbled a few more things I needed to pack or pick up at the store, and looked up at her. "What are you going to do here by yourself while I'm gone?"

She waved me off. "I'll be just fine. I'm always into something. I'll have our heroes over once a week for supper—Maybe twice—and every morning for games. I'll even step outside and play cards with them some. You know I'm busy volunteering at the library now. So don't you worry about me."

But I could hear it in her voice. She was feeling low too.

"Well, I will so worry," I fussed. "And if you don't call me every day, I'll call Peter and check on you."

Yap Yap put his paws on Grandma's knee and begged to be picked up. "Aw, look here." She lifted him into her lap. "See, I've got lots of company."

I reached over and scratched the dog's ears.

"There, there, Coral, I didn't mean to make you sad," she told me. "You'll have enough on your mind trying to learn your way around Charleston. I want you to be happy. Why don't we talk about something pleasant?"

She petted the dog for several minutes while I concentrated on not forgetting anything I needed. Peter was driving me up to school in Charleston day after tomorrow, just to make sure the car made it. Then he'd fly back.

"I've got an idea," she said. "A happy one."

I peeked up at her.

She laid her book in her lap and crossed her arms. "Show me your best wedding dress design. One you'd really want to wear."

"Where did...what are you talking about?"

"Weddings—one of the happiest topics in the world. Humor me."

"I'm not getting married. There's no one in this entire world as great as Grandpa. Nobody."

"Come *onnnnnn*. Humor me."

I rolled my eyes and grinned.

"Wait, wait," she said. "Design me one too—a gown for the grandmother of the bride."

"It's a waste of time, Grandma. There's nobody out there for me. There's absolutely no one."

She raised her eyebrows as if waiting on a real answer.

I gave in. "All right, all right. Only for you, Grandma." I laid aside my list and dug in my bag for a drawing pad. It wasn't because I felt like drawing a wedding gown or planning a wedding. But because I wouldn't see the dearest person in my life for a long, long time. And I wanted to spend every minute I could with her. And I wanted to make her happy.

I could finish my list in the morning. Besides, if I forgot anything, there were plenty of stores in Charleston.

Grandma tweaked my arm and picked up her book again, this time, Marjorie Stoneman Douglas's *River of Grass*.

"I'll be right up the coast, Grandma. And I'll come back a lot. It's just for two years. Remember how the last two flew by?" I was reassuring myself as well as her.

She squeezed my arm again. "Give me those pictures when you're done," was all she said. And from the corner of my eye, I was pretty sure I caught her blinking something back.

A lump formed in my throat. "I'm coming right back after my degree."

But life is full of twists and turns.

Chapter 33

The first year and a half I returned as often as breaks allowed. Grandma never diminished in her sharpness of mind or her appearance. She dressed and fancied herself up in those bright beautiful colors and was the envy of every retired woman at the Baptist church. Her health, her energy, and her faith all remained intact.

Over Christmas break, as usual, I'd flown to Ft. Myers. "Please, don't try to drive it yourself, Coral," she said, repeating her usual speech. "Don't put yourself at risk."

I didn't need prompting, though. I hated the drive.

"Peter can pick you up from the airport," she said. I was glad she wasn't going to pick me up herself.

I was only too happy for Peter's help. As busy as he was with his business and his own family, he could have just as easily sent one of the girls from the office. I still don't know how he arranged to get away, but he did. Priorities, I guess.

This time, as usual, Grandma accompanied him to the airport. She didn't want to miss a minute with me, and I was glad. I didn't want to miss a minute with her. After a joyful airport reunion, we sat in the back seat, jabbering a mile a minute while Peter drove.

"Grandma you're so beautiful," I told her. "But have you lost a few pounds?"

"Oh, posh," she said. "No, I haven't," she said.

"She's had a few headaches," Peter said, his eyes reflecting in the rear-view mirror.

"Have you talked to your doctor?"

"Oh, ya'll quit picking on me now. It's nothing." And she refused to discuss it any further.

From that point on, she turned the conversation around and fussed and quizzed me about all my own health and eating habits.

A mile or so down the road she got a sparkle in her eye. "I've got to show you something," she said. "But first—" She reached forward and tapped Peter on the shoulder of his suit coat. "Peter, would you mind? And take us on that little detour I mentioned?"

He winked into the mirror.

"But let's stop by and get a cone first."

Well, if she wanted to stop by that old ice cream place, I wasn't going to be the one to spoil her fun.

"Let's not go in," she said, "just drive by the window. Thank you."

Well, at least we wouldn't linger.

"But that's not my surprise," she added, pointing a finger at me.

We got our cones, and Peter turned down the exact same side street where I knew we'd pass that old white building. *Oh, no. Why would she want to drive by that sad old thing? Especially at Christmas. Must be heading past it to something else.*

I licked my cone as we approached the corner clump of trees and braced myself for a view of that horrid *Unwanted Pregnancies* sign.

We cleared the trees. But instead of that peeling white building, there stood an inviting and transformed doll-house of a place. Peter slowed. A bright yellow sign read *Christian Counseling Services.*

I almost dropped my cone. "Whoa, slow down, Peter," I said, staring at the transformation. I turned to Grandma, who beamed. She could hardly contain herself.

"Peter. Could you pull in, please, over here?" I indicated the parallel parking space on the right. I wanted to take a better look. *What a change.*

Rolling down our windows we peered out. My gaze drifted over to the sidewalk.

"Remember that day?" I said. "You anointed the sidewalk."

Rosella caught a drip of chocolate with her lips. "Precisely. How could I forget?"

After a few minutes I'd seen enough. "I guess we can go now."

She eyed me with a knowing grin. "God answered my prayer, Coral. He answered it, the one I'd been praying for a long, long time."

It had been forever. But I'd never thought about joining her to pray them out of business.

"It didn't happen right away. Like I've always told you, we have to keep knocking on God's door."

And that wasn't the only topic Grandma had been knocking on God's door about. There was her son. Shame on me for being so distracted with all my studies. Though I'd given my word, I'd often forgotten to pray for him. Her only son. Her life-long grief.

And here, she'd taken up my grief like it was her own and never let up. Never forgotten. She put me to shame.

Shame on me. So then and there I made a decision to do better about praying for her son.

Lord, save that man, draw him to You and straighten him out.
Please do it in time for Rosella to see.

Then a nagging reminder in my heart about her recent weight loss and headaches prompted me further. *And one more thing Lord, please keep her healthy while I'm away.*

After Christmas I returned to Charleston's Galena University.

Little did I know that while I sailed through my semester— loving every project, test, and assignment in fashion design and writing and savoring them as food for my soul—Grandma's health had been steadily declining.

And she'd hidden it well.

Exam week arrived. And I was looking forward to spending my summer in Ft. Myers.

But it also brought a dreadful phone call from Peter.

Chapter 34

I gripped the phone. "Please tell me Grandma's still alive," I said. "I just talked to her a few days ago. It was the first time I'd let the pressures of studying keep me from calling every night. I'd skipped one single night.

"I knew she'd been tired. But how could she suddenly be so sick with a UTI and sepsis? And in the hospital?"

I slumped against the women's restroom wall with the phone pressed tight against my ear. I hoped nobody came in. Peter should have called me when they'd first taken her to the hospital. Not just before my class. Why had it taken him so long to call me? And he hadn't bothered to explain or offer an apology. It wasn't like him.

I was feeling very guilty right now.

"Let me talk to her," I insisted. "I need to hear her voice."

But she was asleep, he'd said. No need to disturb her. And I should not worry, according to Peter. Just pray for her. The doctors said she was going to be fine.

He should have called me right away. Grandma was all I had.

My imagination revved into overdrive.

I pictured a cluster of medics working frantically over her frail body.

Had they shocked her like on one of those horrible TV shows?

I had to know. My fears spilled into the phone.

"Did Grandma die and come back to life?"

"Of course not." I knew he was trying to be patient, but I could hear his exasperation.

"What is it you're not telling me, Peter?"

"Stop it, Coral. It's not like that at all. You're letting your imagination run away with you."

A writer with an imagination is a good thing, but as a natural worry-wart I'd often been accused of letting it run away with me.

He took a deep breath. "Your grandma's recovery is under control. She's better and stronger. Her fever's down. There's no need to put off any of your exams to come down," he told me.

But I needed to see her face to face. Or hear her voice. *Now.* Charleston International Airport was only a hop away from Galena.

"I could be there before lunch. All my professors would understand," I pleaded.

As the family attorney Peter held my purse strings. "I'm sure they would," he said. He cleared his throat. I imagined him right now glancing at his watch, needing to get down to the courthouse.

The pause gave him just enough time to put his answer into diplomatic terms. "I'll get your plane ticket for Saturday."

So here I was.

Stuck.

With my little red Mustang—that he advised couldn't be trusted for such a long trip. I wondered if that was just his and Grandma's excuse to keep me safe and off the highway.

I pictured Grandma's IVs and tubes and replayed our last conversation. Actually, this whole thing might be my fault. The last time we talked I hadn't had the sense to know how sick she was. She *had* complained of being a little tired... I should have notified Peter.

And what had the both of us noticed back in December? About her weight and such? I should have paid more attention. That was quite a while back, but maybe it was connected.

A day or two ago when I last spoke to her she'd sounded so— normal. So happy. It didn't make sense how she could have been so sick all of a sudden like this.

"I should have seen something coming," I told Peter. "This is all my fault."

"No worries there, Coral. She'd never let you or *anyone else* know she if she was sick. She'd just take care of it."

Grandma always took good care of herself. And never complained. "But..."

"It was just a little more than her body could handle, and it got the best of her."

My phone wasn't on speaker, yet his voice echoed in the otherwise silent room.

He was right, I knew. I guess Grandma hadn't realized how sick she was, either. Until it was almost too late. She'd never neglect herself.

"We're keeping a close eye on her. We're with her at the hospital several times a day."

Peter's wife, Dolly, probably.

Peter's voice returned. "'Stay in school, Coral,' she told me. Those are your grandma's exact words, 'And wrap up the semester well.' She had some big plans for you all this summer. And still has them."

I'd rather she tell me that herself. Could she even talk?

Such lousy timing.

Not a way to enter my finals week.

I took a deep breath.

We said good-bye, but not before Peter reminded me *again* of his earlier call, before she was sick, when he'd asked me to make that first move and introduce myself to Matt, Sol's son and hence, Grandma's real flesh and blood grandson. *Arghh!* Right now, this guy Matt was the last person I wanted to talk to. With Grandma sick now, I thought Peter would have just forgotten about Matt and let it slide. But here he was, *again*, reminding me to call the guy.

What a huge negative distraction. I wanted to concentrate on Grandma, and spend time researching sepsis and UTIs—not on some lame conversation with Matt who I'd never met and didn't care to meet. Ever.

There were too many unanswered questions. I know Grandma'd almost *died*. One of our friends—my *uncles*—found her passed out in bed. But how long had she lain there? Poor little Grandma Rosella. And how bad off was she?

For a long minute, I leaned against the tiles feeling my heartbeat and listening to the sounds of my breathing and imagining the brutal things she might have endured.

For the millionth time I wished she had gone ahead and adopted me—she'd practically raised me after all—then I could truly say she was my grandma. I tried not to let it bother me, but it still did—getting brushed off about adoption those eight years ago. It still didn't seem fair.

Even now, the law didn't care how old I was. I'd done the research. Twenty years old or not, I could still be adopted. Yet this was no time to bring all that up.

Nevertheless, the point was, adoption would mean I *belonged* right now.

The process wouldn't have cost her much. Not with Peter Cordero in the family.

I would have gladly paid her back. Even double.

Yet her generosity wasn't the issue. All my expenses—college and every little thing I ever needed or wanted—had been gladly supplied by Grandma Rosella.

And now, what I dreaded—nearly as much as those upcoming tests—was having to make this next call to introduce myself to Mateo, or *Matt*. Her *real* grandson.

Hence Peter's reminders this morning over the phone.

"Not *him*, Peter," I had begged. "You do it for me. I don't want anything to do with Sol's offspring."

None whatsoever. Sol was wicked and hateful. *Not* a good character. I was well aware of his ways and the way he spoke to Rosella over the phone.

His son Matt would be the same.

Peter had ignored my protestations and kept on talking. "It's important for you to get in touch with Matt, get to know him a little before the meeting, and stay in communication with him. Then when you come down, the three of us will meet down here in Ft. Myers."

Oh, crumb. This weekend. Saturday. We had one week to get acquainted. "But…"

"Your Grandma's directions, Coral. Straight from her. She has her reasons."

"Peter…"

"Do you trust me?"

I couldn't respond. He knew my answer.

"I asked you something, Coral. Do. You. Trust. Me?"

"Well, yes…"

"Good. Then please, don't argue. It's very important to Grandma Rosella."

And that was that.

There was nothing more to say on that call except good-bye. We hung up, more than a little irritated with each other.

Worse yet, and more alarming now at this juncture, that meeting Peter had planned for us had something to do with Grandma's estate planning. Matt and I were to be co-successor trustees.

A chill ran through me.

Too much like death. It gave me the heebie-jeebies.

I didn't want a meeting. I didn't care two hoots about the estate planning.

All I wanted to do was *see* her.

And prove she was alive. And know that she was going to be okay.

Peter had assured me—*told* me—she'd recover. But—*co-successor trustees?* The term sounded like a *finality*. And I didn't want to talk about her death.

I squeezed my eyes shut. What if Grandma had actually died?

And Peter was covering it up?

Maybe this was all a ploy to get me through the semester without freaking out.

"Please, Lord. No." I blew out a breath and pushed away from the bathroom wall. There was not a thing I could do right now—other than to trust old Peter and hope for the best.

So I scrolled through Peter's prior texts and located Matt's contact info.

My exam was only two doors down the hall. As I exited, I transferred his information into my contacts. I'd be needing it frequently in the next few days.

I formed a picture of Sol's pale face and balding, curly hair in my mind—like the photo on Grandma's refrigerator, and paused outside the classroom door. I hit the *edit* command on Matt's info. Ha! Why not give him a suitable nickname? Students filtered around me as I altered his name to *Matt the Rat*. He had to be as hateful as his dad Sol, right?

I tried to think of a nice way to introduce myself. "Oh, hi, I'm Coral the neighbor, and co-executor of your grandma's estate…"

Nah, he'd probably bark something back, like, "You've got to be kidding." I couldn't help but superimpose on him the nasal tone of his dad's narcissistic speech. I'd overheard it so many times via Grandma's phone—even when she wasn't on speaker. I imagined Matt's voice like it saying, *"Grandma named you co-executor and you're just a neighbor? A dad-gum neighbor? So who thought up that joke?"*

A twinge of guilt snagged my thoughts, and I lowered the device. It wasn't very fair of me to make assumptions about his character like this.

But then, I had to prepare myself. What was that phrase—chip off the old block? Like father, like son? Had to be some truth to it.

This was way awkward—me, the stranger, an intruder, introducing myself.

For the first time in years, the sting of being called Grandma's little trailer-trash neighbor returned. The words still stung. Never mind that poem about sticks and stones, it wasn't true.

Now Matt would probably call me that, too, especially now with me sticking my nose into his family's business. Co-successor trustees. *Pfft!* That's what he'd think.

I wished he understood Grandma's and my relationship.

Standing outside the classroom door I found his info again. I poised my thumb over the call button. Wait. Why not text? Then he wouldn't be able to yell. Or call me names.

Here goes nothing. I tapped out the letters.

```
Hi, Matt. Did Peter the lawyer ever
get in touch with you???
```

Oh, shoot. That came out all backwards. So much for planning. I hit send anyway.

His fast response told me he must have been holding his phone.

```
Who is this?
```

I glanced through the classroom door. Still no teacher. This professor was frequently late.

> I'm Coral. Your grandma's neighbor
> girl.

I might as *well* say neighbor girl. Matt never visited his Grandma Rosella. He wouldn't know I was more like her adopted grand-daughter than a neighbor. He probably didn't know I actually lived in Rosella's house, or that I called her Grandma, ate her food, and loved her like my own nana.

And Grandma Rosella *loved me*.

Yes, she did.

The term *neighbor girl* was good enough for now.

> ys

I guess that meant yes that Peter got in touch with him. Not even a hello.

> Matt, I'm sorry about your grandma.
> ty

He ought to be comforting *me*.

I added a little sad-face emoji.

> My heart's worried. Worried to pieces.

Probably too much information. Not that Matt cared about that, of course. Once again, I leaned inside the classroom—peeked all the way to the back of the room. Had I missed the professor coming in? Students were seated. Still no instructor. All the same, though, I ought to go on in.

I glanced down at the phone's screen. Hmmm. How could I phrase this next one to see what he knows? I typed

> I think I understand this co-succes-
> sor trustee thing.

His abrupt response was no more than three stupid little text bubbles.

> basic
> agree and sign
> call me

He couldn't even use periods. *Smarty britches.*

The automatic door whooshed at the far end of the building and our professor stepped inside with a roll of papers under his arm—our test, of course.

I typed fast.

```
Can't right now. Heading into a final
exam. We'll talk later.
```

Two more text bubbles from him.

```
              ditto
              call
```

Bossy Butt. I had no desire to call him. Why couldn't he call me? I turned off the phone and threw it in my purse.

Inside the classroom I found a seat near the windows. Made up my mind to be even more grammatical with my texts. After all I was a creative writing and design major. He was probably some kind of business jerk like his dad.

As I settled in, I wondered where Matt attended school or what he studied. I'd inquired, but Grandma wouldn't discuss him. Didn't even have his picture on the fridge. I'd never understood that.

Why did she not have a photo of her own grandson on her fridge?

Maybe he looked even *worse* than I imagined. Disfigured or something. Maybe he was so hateful like his dad she couldn't put up his picture.

This much I'd always known—we were the same age. And… Grandma had told me he was a student now like me.

My attitude settled down as the chatter around me quieted. Right now, I had to clear my mind or suffer a disaster on this final exam.

I took a few deep breaths. Got myself under control again. It was dumb to have gotten so riled up about Matt the grandson. He hadn't done anything to deserve it.

Truth was, maybe I was a little jealous—a sin, I knew—for he *was* the *real relative.* A true grandson. And I repented silently for feeling that way.

Truth was, for all my wanting-to-be, I was no blood-relation at all. Rosella just wasn't my family.

Chapter 35

After the test I headed out to get some fresh air and find a bench where I could study for the next one. Two exams today. The last three were all on Friday.

But the dread of that co-successor trusteeship thing with Matt hovered over me. I didn't want to deal with anyone like his father, Sol.

One thing Rosella had always made clear to me—she didn't want Sol involved in her business affairs.

Yes, Sol deserved to know his mother was sick and in the hospital, but I hoped Peter was keeping him out of the loop for a few more days. Surely, Peter would see to that.

Once Sol found out she was sick, we'd have another problem. He'd be circling Ft. Myers like a vulture. Hoping she'd…

I shook my head and scolded myself. Of course, I should stop worrying. Surely Peter had Sol under control.

"If and when I die," Rosella had said, "which I'm sure won't happen for a very long time, you have to fly home and manage the funeral. I've arranged it. You and Peter will manage it. But please keep Sol out of it. That's my only request, and *very* important to me." She shook her finger and repeated, "Sol will get his inheritance, his *money*. But keep him out of it."

I tried to pry more out of her.

"I wouldn't be surprised if Sol tried to squeeze out a few more dollars by donating my body to forensics," she added. "He can't seem to get enough of that stuff. Don't be money-hungry when you grow up, Coral."

"I won't," I told her. "Never."

Of course, Sol didn't need to be greedy. He had all the money in the world. He was rolling in dough from his legalized CBD sales and shady friends.

After all she'd told me about Sol, and all I'd picked up through the phone, I wondered if he had even stolen things.

"I still love my son, Coral. But he won't listen to me. Please tell me you'll pray for his soul. *I* pray for it. Everyday."

So I did.

I guess there's a difference between recognizing a person's true character and forgiving them. And then caring for their soul.

I had trouble with the forgiving and the caring.

Especially the way he neglected his mother. She didn't deserve that treatment.

Help him, Lord. For Rosella's sake. Please save him. Make him nice. But keep him away from me. And don't let him get involved in her business right now.

I shuddered to think I had to deal with his son now. "You have to," Peter had said.

And one more thing, Lord. Please help me get this communication and meeting thing with Matt done and over with. Quick. In Jesus name, Amen.

I left Building C where most of my classes were and headed down the steps. My body was stiff and sore from bending over my books and drawing board all weekend with no breaks.

My final project for Fashion Design had been the pattern-rendering of Grandma's formal dress. Grandma, a year and a half ago had mentioned her desire for a grandmother-of-the-bride dress. Why she'd ask for such a thing I had no idea. But I'd created a design for it. On Friday, I'd do a short classroom talk and present the sketches to the class and my professor, all at the same time for a pass/fail grade and comments from my peers.

I'd created a pattern, but I'd have to take a class next term where it would be my final project. I imagined this dress would be a sunset-colored style in flowing chiffon, graceful skirts, and an over-the-shoulder sweep of silk roses. Since Grandma was all about color, she would love this combination of all her favorites.

I passed by the library and headed toward the student union. At midpoint stood the awning-covered vending area where I'd find a much-needed soda. The pond, down the shady slope to my left, was my favorite fair-weather study place. Scattered across its lawn were several benches and tables, the nearest only a dozen steps away from the machines.

Once again, my mind reeled as I considered my recent calls from Peter.

At least Grandma was alive. And getting better.

I wanted to talk to her. But Peter had said no, she needs her rest. So I fought off the urge to dial her up.

"Will she be home by the end of the week when I return?"

"The doctor's hoping for Saturday morning sometime," Peter said.

Okay. So maybe he was telling the truth.

At the vending area, I set my books on the concrete with my straw purse leaning against them, its large silk rose facing out. I always wore matching flowers, one in my hair, and one on my purse, a nod to Grandma and her unique style. Like Grandma, I switched out the colors, according to my dress. I loved dresses. Summer sundresses especially. Anything bright.

I plugged my quarters into the soda machine and checked my texts. Not a thing from Matt the Grandson.

Good.

Once again I wondered where old Matt went to school.

My phone in my purse vibrated, and as I dropped a can of soda in beside it I peeked at the screen. Peter again.

I lifted it out. "Is she still okay?"

He laughed. "Fine, fine. Stop worrying."

"One more important question," I said. "Have you told Sol about any of this?"

"You know, I thought about it. Since she's getting better, we'll keep him out of the picture until you two get down here."

We meant me and old Mateo the grandson. *Matt Flores.*

I pulled my tote over my shoulder, adjusted my books, and headed for the benches. It was only fair to inform Sol. But still… "What if Sol finds out before he should?"

"Stop worrying, Coral. And Matt definitely won't tell him. Just finish the semester and give me a call."

What did he mean, *Matt definitely wouldn't tell him*? "Wait, don't hang up," I said. I pressed the phone against my heart and eased myself and the books onto a bench. I stared across the water without even seeing it. I pictured Rosella alone in her bed, half-dead and alone.

Tears welled in my eyes. *Poor dear Rosella.*

I lifted the phone to my ear again. Peter was still there. "I need you to tell me everything."

He waited a minute before answering. "I didn't want these details to worry you. She did get a little out of her head with the fever and all. But that's down. The medication is causing her to sleep a lot. They want her resting."

I stifled a sob with my knuckles. No wonder he didn't want me to talk to her.

"I didn't spill that to make you worry."

Grandma. I pictured her head with those angel braids against her pillow.

I turned the phone away and swiped my wrist across my tears.

And now with this meeting, this co-executor thing—I was doomed to be labeled an intruder. By father and son. I didn't need that kind of stress.

"Are you still there?" Peter asked.

I sniffed and nodded. Not that he could see me.

"It's hard, I know," he said. "Rosella's been your anchor. You going to be okay?"

I couldn't answer.

"We're here for you. And we're all family. The heroes. Me. You. All our friends. We're not going anywhere."

I knew all that, but still… I couldn't respond.

Peter waited patiently. I knew he didn't think me weird. He understood me. The whole family had been through so much over the years.

"Who-who f-found…?" Thank goodness they *had.* I'd never asked him that, and now I couldn't get the words out.

"Tio Ignacio and the uncles found her. They came to play cards, and she didn't come out. They were all there. All of the uncles."

Thank goodness, they'd come every day. Oh, I missed them so much. I couldn't wait till Saturday.

I wiped the wet phone on my dress. "Tell Grandma and everyone else I love them, Peter, but I-I have to go now."

Here I was, miles and miles from home with no way in the world to help except follow some vague instructions.

It felt so neglectful.

I slid the phone into my purse and pulled out my notes for the next test.

And hoped I could study.

Chapter 36

T alk to you later, Pete." Matt Flores clicked off the phone and set it beside him on the stairwell of the Student Union Building. Good thing the place had cleared out. "Man," he whispered as he slid his palms down his face. He'd only spoken with Grandma two days ago. She couldn't be sick. Not that sick.

"I should catch a flight down right now," he'd told Pete.

"No. Stay and wrap things up. Then you're free and clear for semester break. And hopefully a summer break. *Then* spend some time down here. You'll have nothing hanging over you. But right now, Grandma doesn't want your studies disrupted."

Disrupted? They already were.

And as Grandma's spokesperson, Peter had relayed the plan for the meeting—and that bunch of craziness about her neighbor girl, Coral.

Not that Matt didn't know who she was. But a neighbor didn't figure into his family's business. Grandma had spoken of her often. Each time he'd visited.

But *he'd* never met her. Hadn't even seen a picture. Never bumped into her. She was always away at camp when he came down.

He'd complained to Peter. "C'mon, a non-relative as co-executor? What an insult." But the man hadn't budged. Grandma's plan was set in stone. Well, then, Matt would just have to see it through.

He stood, picked up his things, and slung his bag over his shoulder.

Coral was nothing as far as family connections went. And she certainly had no business as a co-successor trustee.

Wait till Dad gets wind of this. He'll be steaming, all right. First, that

Grandma hadn't named Sol as a trustee. And second, it wasn't just his son that had displaced him, but him and some neighbor girl.

He imagined Dad's flaming face—veins popping, spittle flying.

As usual, the man would be beside himself.

"Dad. You've lost it this time," Matt would say, "Lost your ever-loving control."

He didn't feel sorry for Sol. And if Dad couldn't handle the facts, Matt would just have to set him straight. "Look, I'm not responsible for Grandma's choices," he'd tell him.

Of course, Dad would yell and demand justice, insist Matt straighten things out. Order Matt to come home. Sign a pile of documents to reverse and manipulate the whole thing.

Demand, demand. Dad's whole MO. And Matt would simply tell him, "No, I won't come home." In fact, Matt planned to *never* go back to that Nevada hell-hole. "And no, I can't override Grandma *or* name you co-executor trustee, or anything else."

Dad would rage for days. Worse, he might even show up in Ft. Myers—a vain show, but one that would be *very* bad. Very ugly.

At least Matt's university was on the opposite side of the continent from Sol.

"Grandma's going to be okay," Peter had said. "And your dad is not to be involved in this meeting with you and Coral. So keep it to yourself. Don't even let on that Grandma's ill."

Matt sighed. "So then why all this co-successor trustee business?"

"Routine preplanning," Peter had said.

Too bad Matt's mom wasn't here to talk to. After she left, she'd made herself scarce. For the last four years Matt didn't even know where she was.

Talk about feeling alone.

Matt shifted his bag and strode through the exit toward vending.

He'd have to set Sol straight. "Please, Dad, just tend to your money-lending business and cannabis shop, and I'll tend to Grandma. She's sick, and I know this fact bugs you, but I guarantee she's alive and getting better." He paused, shook his head, the continued on. "Nope, can't even say that much to Dad."

For once, now that Matt was out from under Dad's roof—for good, he hoped—he'd stand up to him.

Unlike Dad, who was always angry at Grandma, Matt actually cared about her. And wanted her to live. Sol knew nothing about love.

Unfortunate, but true. And Grandma understood that. Yet she didn't hold a grudge.

How could Grandma be the lousy mother she claimed? Matt had never pictured her that way. And yes, people can change. All Matt had ever seen in her was a kind and loving woman.

But she always insisted, "I earned some of Sol's anger, Matt. I truly did."

Chapter 37

own by the pond I checked the time and stood beside my purse and books. It was time for my next class, a test-prep for one of Friday's exams.

A movement by the vending machines caught my eyes. A young man in a wheelchair struggled to maintain his lapful of books as he inserted his money in the soda machine. A straight cast on his leg unbalanced him, and the machine's money-slot was too high. Books slid everywhere.

I rushed his way. "Here, let me help you." We stacked everything back on his lap. My experiences with Grandpa Eduardo had left a soft spot in my heart for people in wheelchairs.

But any decent person would have helped this poor guy.

"Thanks. I'm not used to this chair yet." His cast did look new.

"That's okay. Let me get your drink."

"Dr. Pepper," he said, and wheeled toward the nearest table. "I'll park over here so I can study a while."

I plugged in his coins. "Anything else I can help with before class? I've got about a minute," I said as I brought the drink over. I cleared off some acorns and a muffin-wrapper for him as I set it down.

"Nope, thank you very much, all set for now." He pulled out his own brown bag, well-worn and a little squished. "Thank you again."

"Okay, then."

"Ha," he said, sort of as an afterthought, and raised one finger as if to make a point. "You ever heard of that Bible verse about not being forgetful to entertain strangers? That some have entertained angels unawares." His eyes twinkled.

I laughed and waved him off. *Good joke.* He certainly didn't look like an angel. "I was happy to help you. No problem at all."

As I retrieved my purse and books from the nearby table, a fleeting thought passed through my mind. But it vaporized as I turned back to the soda machines and caught my breath.

There, leaning against the machines and gazing straight at me, stood a student I'd never seen before, and dangerous-handsome. He grinned—that same amazing cheek-creasing smile I'd seen in only one person—my dear hero, Grandpa Eduardo. God rest his soul. I gaped for one shocked moment at the guy's melted-chocolate eyes, his faint stubble—and I turned, probably too fast, to scurry off to Building C.

Who was *that*?

At the top of the steps, Building C's door swooshed open, and I dared to turn—to check on my new wheelchair friend, I told myself—but also to shake off that lingering sensation of being stared at.

But there they remained—the both of them, exactly as I'd left them, returning my gaze.

I waved. They waved.

Not that I had time to think about it right now, but where had the good-looking one been hiding all semester?

Was he even a student?

I tried to review the scene, to call up whether he even carried a backpack.

But all I could see were those handsome dimples.

Matt paused a beat. As soon as the girl with the flower stepped inside the door of Building C, he headed over to the guy in the wheelchair. *Might as well solve this puzzle right now.* "Nice girlfriend you got there."

"I wish."

Yes!

"You happen to catch her name?"

The guy in the wheelchair laughed and opened a baggie full

of broken cookies. "Never thought to ask her. All I know is she needed to get to class.

Matt gave him a nod and stepped away.

His lucky day.

Chapter 38

It was only May, but the heat already felt like summer in Charleston, and I was already suffocating, even in my sundress. The air conditioning in Building C had been cranked down and felt good on my skin. Goosebumps ran along the freckles of my arm, and I tightened my grip on my books.

My fair skin was nothing like doughy old Sol's. He'd sent us a recent newspaper clipping of him earning an award for some great accomplishment and shaking some other old guy's hand. I'd never met Sol, only heard him on the phone, but by that picture I could tell he'd gone to pot. *Ha! Literally.*

I tried to picture Matt who would probably look just like his dad—ugly-pale with a curly scruff of dirty-blond hair—and a premature bald patch. I shuddered. That, of course, was based on Rosella's old refrigerator-photo. And Sol would be gray by now. In some small ways he did resemble his mom—Grandma Rosella—but those nasty traits of his divided the two like the sides of the Grand Canyon.

Bad character ruins good looks. I'd have to write that down in my book of proverbs and great sayings.

A plume of regret passed across the back of my mind. Once again, I needed to repent of negative thoughts. What a battle this was becoming, pushing down those thoughts. I should be praying for Sol, like Rosella had asked me, instead of thinking like this about him.

Nonetheless, I determined then and there that Matt and I should get through our introductions over the phone—to minimize our contact.

What advice had Rosella always given me? *Stay positive.* Well, I planned to try, but Rosella and her influence were so far away. Except for Peter, I was cut off from her, the uncles, and little Yap Yap the dog.

How *was* that little squirt?

I hoped Peter was taking good care of him.

Then Sol's image returned like a bad dream.

I couldn't seem to get him out of my thoughts.

For the millionth time I recalled Grandma's warning. "Don't allow Sol to get involved with my personal business," she'd said. "Or I'll be stuck in a nursing home for sure."

I'd never let that happen.

Chapter 39

Matt, with an hour of study ahead of him, proceeded to the library. Building C sat right next to it, and he knew just the spot upstairs where he could study and watch for the girl whenever she came out.

Unless she left by the back door.

He shook his head. Chances were, she'd leave the same way she entered. Too bad he couldn't clone himself.

Sandy Beach. That's what he called her. It's what she reminded him of, anyway. At least until he could learn her name.

It seemed unfair to call her *that girl.*

He'd captured a solid mental image of her, and reviewed it as he walked. Those freckles, those blue eyes…the way she'd stood there in the sun just now, the breeze lifting strands of her long hair about her face and flower, the way she'd looked right back at him—with the pond glimmering behind her.

A picture so lovely.

His imaginings dissolved as he entered the air-conditioned world of the library and headed upstairs, two steps at a time.

The spring term was closing down fast. If he didn't meet his Sandy Beach this week, he could lose his chance forever. This could be her final semester.

He *had* to meet her. Get a good look at that ring finger.

One can only hope.

For Matt, the next forty-five minutes passed like a geriatric snail. Studying was useless. This was no time to lose himself in his notes. He'd have to study later.

His phone on the table vibrated, and he checked the screen just to lay it back down again. *Coral,* the screen said.

Sorry, kiddo. Bad timing. For now, anyway.

The class bell was about to ring. And when it did, he didn't want to miss when Sandy Beach exited that door right down there.

He picked up the phone again and stood. On the other hand, shouldn't he answer? Coral the neighbor girl might have important news.

With his eyes on the front door to Building C, he gave in and clicked the green button anyway. "Hello?"

At that exact moment the front door slid open downstairs. And there, on the front steps appeared his beautiful Sandy Beach with that flower in hair and—hey, a matching one on her purse. He hadn't noticed that before—very classy—and—*uh oh*—a phone against her ear.

A sour feeling gripped his gut. There could be a boyfriend.

Sandy Beach paused on the top step—obviously out of class early. If he hurried, he could get down there before she walked off.

In the meantime, the bell rang. Class was over. Within seconds students would be thronging the halls. He stole one more glimpse of Sandy Beach through the window and eyed the stairs as he applied the phone to his ear.

"Uh, Coral, could we talk later? I'm—I'm kinda in the middle of something. Sorry."

"But, I…"

He hung up anyway, reached across the table, grabbed his books, and headed downstairs. Students already clogged the stairwell, and he wove his way through and around them, lunging two steps at a time, whenever he could.

At the front door he dodged another group and almost fell over his wheelchair friend.

"Hey, man…" the guy said, clearly wanting to engage him.

Matt paused long enough to pat him on the shoulder. "Sorry, man, I'll catch up with you later. Gotta hurry." He felt bad about that, but this was important. Very important. He rounded the corner and his lungs deflated. *Noooo! Where'd she go?*

She couldn't disappear this quick. She just couldn't. He tightened his grip on the books and took off straight ahead. Glanced left and right.

Nothing. The parking lot to the right revealed no white dress with bright pink flowers. She couldn't have gone *that* far, anyway. Unless she ran.

The parking lot to the left was around a corner. Off he sprinted.

He paused long enough behind Building C to scan the parking lot. Nothing.

Chapter 40

After class, Coral headed straight for the north parking lot. Time to get home and change shoes. Matt's rudeness on the phone didn't help matters.

As she strode across the asphalt, she replayed the scene at the soda machine in her mind and the strange comment by the guy in the wheelchair...

That's when the most fragile of memories crept to the forefront of her brain like a forgotten dream.

The smell.

Like a cloud of roses. There at the soda machine. Too strong to be her imagination.

And not one rose grew on this campus.

How odd.

The last time this happened was when she escaped Mama's brute male friend at the back door of their trailer.

And then another lost memory resurfaced.

She'd smelled it when Mama died.

Oh, yes, there were those awful smells of death and blood that filled the room.

But there was that other one. Clearly different.

And it also filled the room. *Roses.*

Coral shuddered and pushed it out of her mind as she moved across the pavement to the trunk of her car.

Chapter 41

Matt gazed across the left parking lot…yes, yes, yes!

There she was, putting things in her trunk. A red car.

Matt took off running. But what would he say to her? This was the weirdest thing he'd ever done—chasing down a girl to meet her.

But Matt couldn't care less about being ashamed.

Wait, what if he scared the girl?

The thought had barely formed when, "*Ooof!*" Matt flew forward. His chest slammed into the grass. "*Unnngghhhh!*" Stars flickered behind his eyes. His books slid, twirled, and grated over the asphalt beyond. Papers spilled everywhere. Facedown, Matt's ankles hung over a cable. Its small sign, *Keep off the Grass,* dug into the very sod it protected.

Daggers of pain shot through Matt's chest as he clutched his ribs, winced, and rolled over to free his feet from the cable.

"Oh, man, that smarts." Up on his knees he crawled.

The girl.

He stood. Tottered there. Unable to move and barely able to breathe as Sandy Beach, oblivious to it all, drove away in the opposite direction in a little red Mustang with a Florida tag.

Chapter 42

By late Friday all my creative writing tests and fashion design projects were complete. Back at my apartment, I parked the car and breathed a sigh. Four days had slipped by without me calling or texting Matt again. The word avoidance flickered across my mind and left behind a plume of guilt. I wondered if Matt would even try to keep his end of the deal with Peter.

Too bad Matt and I couldn't just wait and meet down in Ft. Myers and forget all this getting-to-know-you stuff.

Whatever. I'd give him a little more space to take his rightful turn at calling. But right now, it was time for a hot shower. Then I'd start packing for tomorrow's flight.

As I came out of the shower, a twinge of shame assaulted me as I eyed my silent phone on the bed.

Peter hadn't mentioned Matt in his last few calls. He'd trusted me. Way too much. And now I'd let him down. He'd be so disappointed.

Rats. I ought to make some kind of effort.

So with the suitcase open, I texted while I packed.

    Matt, hi. Sorry I haven't called.
    I've been so busy with my exams...But
    we need to do our homework and get to
    know each other.

A whole three minutes passed before he answered.

    Hi. Ys

Arrrrgh! Okay, maybe he was busy. It was obvious he wasn't putting much effort into this yet. We needed to hurry it up. I typed.

> So can you text right now? Are you
> done with your exams?

Again, another long wait. It *was* Friday. Maybe he was out on a date, or doing something like—packing suitcases for tomorrow. Had to be. He responded

> Ys.

Well, finally. I tapped a little more.

> Why don't we start with our majors?
> Mine is creative writing and fashion
> design. What is yours?

As usual, he wasted no extra effort on his answer.

> Bz admin n Entrepreneur-
> ship.

Whatever that was. And that answer didn't take as long to arrive. *Hmm. Signs of his father. Eager when the subject pertains to himself.*

I moved to a new topic, hoping to draw him out.

> I'm sorry we never met. I was wonder-
> ing why you never came to visit your
> Grandpa Eduardo and Grandma Rosella.

No answer. I guess it wasn't really a question. He wanted more?

> We missed you guys at Grandpa Edu-
> ardo's funeral. I wish you and your
> parents had come down. It was beauti-
> ful. Many people attended. There were
> lots of flowers.

Grandma and I sent thank you cards for all the flowers. And I didn't recall a florist's card from Sol. But I could have missed it. Maybe Grandma wrote the thank you for that one.

> I vstd
>
> Bt nt fnrl

He visited—but not the funeral? Two text bubbles again instead of punctuation. Matt definitely had a clear pattern going.

This was tiring, carrying the whole conversation on my own. I took the time to iron up some clothes for my trip. My phone eventually timed out and its screen turned black. It was his turn to make an effort.

In this short time, I had learned one trait about Matt—one he didn't share with his dad.

I was certain that at no time did Matt ever come down to visit his Grandma Rosella.

And that made Matt a liar.

Half an hour later my phone rang. I checked the screen. Well! Old Matt had actually called me for a change. "Hello?"

Matt, on the other end, was laughing.

Are you kidding? His dad never, ever laughed, about anything.

"Yeah, hello there. I didn't really mean to dial you." Another chuckle. "I meant to hit *send message.*"

He actually sounded pleasant.

I wasn't going to be mistaken for a sour pickle, either. I grinned and had to try hard to sound as nice as he did. "I've done that too. Several times. But I hung right up."

"Guess I wasn't quick enough."

I couldn't believe the Jekyll and Hyde contrast between his texts and voice.

Those long pauses before answering my texts—I guessed he didn't want to talk. Maybe he still didn't.

"What are you up to?" I asked. "I bet you're packing."

"In a little while," he said. "But now, about this get-to-know-you assignment from Peter—what were you and I saying in those last texts?"

"I totally forgot, Matt." I teased. "There was such a *looong tiiiiime* between each of your responses."

"Sorry about that. I'm actually driving around and can't text unless I'm stopped."

"Oh, gee," I said. "I don't want you wrecking." And I meant it.

"I hate texting. Hate it."

Maybe it was a guy thing. At least Matt was trying. I definitely wouldn't mind talking to him again. If *this* is who he was.

"But we can talk a minute now."

"Okay, then, Matt, where were we? Oh. I was telling you how lovely the funeral was."

"Everybody loved Grandpa Eduardo," he said.

"I know." There would never be another like him. "His good nature, his humor. Even as a mute, he had personality. Somebody broke the mold after God made him."

He agreed. "Nothing was ever the same at Grandma's after he died."

I nodded my head—of course Matt couldn't see me. "I sure miss him." I couldn't help wondering how Matt would know it was never the same if he hadn't been there in the first place.

Then an old memory leaped out and landed on me. Those little boy's clothes in Grandma's hassock. About my size. All with tags. Wasn't Grandma shipping them? I'd just assumed that. He could have visited. But when? I was there every day and never saw Matt.

I decided to give him a little grace. For now.

I dug into our topic again. "Well, I asked why your family didn't come to the funeral."

"Hmm. Let's save that one for later."

"Well, okay, then." But I wouldn't forget.

We talked a while about our tests. We'd both had late ones this afternoon. Mine sounded so easy. All his sounded so technical. I hardly understood some of his terms. So glad I didn't have his studies.

He has to be brilliant.

Matt wasn't asking me any questions, so I pressed on. "I remember the morning your Grandpa Eduardo died. It was so sad. I was asleep in my room. Your grandma came in and shook my arm. She said, 'Eduardo's gone.' I couldn't quite comprehend. Had he left on a trip?"

I seemed to have Matt's full attention so I went on. "There was no way she could have meant it the *other* away. Not my—" I stopped mid-sentence, not sure what to call Eduardo. I couldn't quite call him *my grandpa* or *Grandpa Eduardo*—not under the circumstances. So I repeated what I'd called him before, "not your Grandpa Eduardo." I rushed on to the next sentence. "And your grandma was so broken hearted. I-I'd never seen her like that."

On the other end, Matt got very quiet. Something had changed.

"Did I say something wrong? I'm sorry, Matt, if that brought up things you don't want to think about."

For another long pause Matt remained silent.

"You still there?" I asked.

"Listen, Coral, still driving. I'll…Let me catch you later." And with that he hung up.

I lowered the phone.

Wow. What did I say?

Chapter 43

Matt frowned at his phone and tossed it into the passenger seat. Well, he'd tried.

The phone landed on his precious check-marked list, which he quickly retrieved.

"I'm done. What a liar."

Why had Peter asked him to get to know this girl? What did it matter? Couldn't Peter just handle that co-successor trusteeship paperwork by himself? Then let them come by and sign off on it?

Matt needed to get back to the business at hand.

His search.

At the red light he flipped to the next page. A realtor had provided him this stack of stapled sheets—names and addresses of all the apartment complexes in Charleston—broken down by city quadrants.

Today was his fourth day and last quadrant. He was almost done.

Thank goodness, straight A's were a breeze for Matt, because this week he'd squandered a good bit of study time and spent it instead checking each property's parking lots for that little red Mustang.

He couldn't afford to lose what might be his last chance to meet his Sandy Beach.

If he didn't find her today, he'd start all over again—at a different time of day.

As he headed down Sam Rittenberg Boulevard he glanced down at the phone. Dared it to ring. He had nothing else to say to that girl Coral.

She'd seemed nice, even decent, up till now. Until she dropped that creative lie on him.

Her bedroom?

The girl had no such thing in Grandma's house.

But boy, could this girl make things sound convincing. If Matt had never been at Grandma's house himself, he would've bought her little story—hook, line, and sinker.

Why would Coral make up such a thing about Grandpa's death?

Sick liar. Opportunist.

And Matt detested liars. They were a dime a dozen in this world.

Actually, *con artist* was more like it. Somehow, this neighbor girl had weaseled her way into Grandma's life.

And Matt wanted her out.

And that's exactly what Matt would demand at Pete's meeting.

At least Coral hadn't asked Matt to meet for coffee, or some other time-waster like that. Between Monday and Friday, she'd sort of dropped off the planet. And at this late stage of the game, he'd no intention of frittering away any more of his precious time on her.

He'd made his effort and now he had scouting to do.

The light turned green, and he stomped the gas. A little too hard. He slowed.

He'd find his Sandy Beach. He'd scout every parking lot in town if he had to.

Coral's four-day gap in that getting-to-know-you thing had bought him precious time to scout the city's apartment complexes for that red Mustang.

He didn't need to get to know the little neighbor girl.

In the morning—Saturday—Matt would catch his flight and get this meeting at Pete's over with. He'd see that Grandma was well and then fly back up here.

Granted, right now he should be doing laundry and packing. But there were only a few more addresses to check off.

He turned the wheel to the right and eased into the next parking lot.

A twinge of guilt passed through his mind. Could he be accused of stalking?

But how else was he going to meet her?

Nah, it wasn't stalking. If she didn't want to meet him, he'd just forget it. He'd drop the subject and leave her alone.

As far as he was concerned, that was not called stalking.

Chapter 44

Ineeded to straighten out this misunderstanding. How were Matt and I supposed to get to know each other if we didn't talk?

Okay, so he didn't want to talk anymore. I'd text. Maybe he'd respond to that. But not if he was driving.

I flopped down in the bedroom chair. *Here goes nothing.* I tapped out my message. I'd give him thirty minutes, enough time to come to a stop somewhere.

> It's Coral again. Sorry to bug you.
> I told Peter I would try to get to
> know you. We can't do it like this.
> Did you tell him you would cooperate?
> There's only one day left.

Half an hour passed.

No response. I needed Matt to get on board. At least a little. I decided to take another stab at it. What was wrong with him?

The only thing that could have possibly upset Matt was my mention of his grandfather.

> I am very sorry my mentioning Eduardo
> upset you.

That woke him up.

> Nope. Room?

What a weird comment. It deserved an explanation.

> What are you talking about?

His response didn't take long.

> Yr rm? Gt rl

I frowned. *Your room?* —Like he was doubting I had a room? And *get real* because he thinks I am a liar?

Sure seemed like it.

I was getting nowhere with this guy.

And my battery was low. I plugged it into the charger and left it on the dresser.

My suitcase was mostly packed by now so I headed outside for fresh air and to water my front yard garden.

My landlord, across the parking lot with her own flower garden, had heard that Grandma was ill and volunteered to treat my garden as her very own while I was away. I was to take all the time I needed. She and my garden would be happy as larks together.

I joked with her that she could do whatever she liked—*Just don't move any gnomes into it.*

She'd laughed and swatted me away.

My garden was tiny but wonderful with its zinnias, marigolds, Dahlberg daisies, cosmos, and portulaca—everything I could possibly cram into that tiny ten by ten space. Between the plants, I'd placed a walkway of flat stones leading to my well-used birdbath.

Most all the other students here had a small patch of plain grass. But I'd petitioned the landlord at the beginning with a design plan and drawing. Considering my two-year lease, she'd given it a chance, and now we were friends.

The only sad thing about my leaving town would be missing my garden.

My plan was to give the soil one last watering and then plug in my timed watering system.

"Grandma," I'd said, after my first quarter here, "everything is perfect in my little garden. But if I come home to Ft. Myers, all my flowers will die. I don't want my landlord to change her mind and tell me I can't have a garden after all."

Grandma took it to heart. "Let me think about it."

And it wasn't long before she mailed me a neatly handprinted paper in someone else's writing. Plans for a watering system.

I called her right away. "Whose plans are these?"

"Remember that young man who designed the lift for your Grandpa Eduardo?" she said.

Absolutely. But she never told me who he was, just that he was my age.

She wasn't ready to tell me that yet. "Well, I explained that there was a young lady in a dilemma—yours, of course—and he came up with this design."

On the paper was my watering system with simple-Simon directions, written in a very unique print. Each lower-case E had a forty-five-degree closure. I'd never seen that before.

"Thank you," I said. "What a hero. This guy is awesome."

In fact, I'd thought so much of this person's kindness, I'd framed and hung the plans on my wall, along with a photo I'd taken of Grandma's trailer and lift. It was a night-shot with all the twinkling lights on under her awning. It reminded me of that first night we'd met. In one corner, I'd placed a gold emblem with the word *Hero* printed in Sharpie.

I had several heroes now.

Whoever designed the lift had enabled my grandparents to continue living in their tiny home. And the watering system saved me from a drab apartment existence without flowers.

After hiring out the electrical work, which Grandma paid for, I set up the timer and emitters myself.

Easy!

I'd like to meet that young man and thank him.

Chapter 45

The quadrants on Matt's list intersected a mile from the university. He folded his paper. This next-to-the-last address was on the opposite side from where he'd started his search four days ago.

So far, he'd struck out. No Sandy Beach. And no red Mustang. At least none with Florida plates.

As he pulled through the next complex's entryway between two very tall sabal palms, he considered the second phase of his search plan. Phase One had all been done in late afternoon. For the next phase, when he returned from Ft. Myers, he'd try mornings.

He'd never give up.

Beyond the trees he turned right and coasted between two rows of cars. At the end he made a one-eighty and headed down to the left end. An elderly lady waved at him. The sign at her place said *Office*. He smiled and returned her wave. Nothing here, either.

But as he passed a large blue SUV he nearly choked on his gum. *Red! Red Mustang.* It was all he could do not to stomp the brakes or floor the gas.

And Florida plates.

His knees trembled.

Act cool. Now what?

He coasted past the scene before he could digest it all.

But there she was, in jeans and a gardening hat, watering a flower garden.

Now what? Now what? Now what?

He hadn't planned his next step. Before he could think straight, he'd reached the end of the unit. "Help me, God. What should I say?"

He did a three-point turn, and there he braked, out of sight behind a truck.

The steering wheel rattled beneath his grip. Anything more and his heart would leap out of his chest. He'd found her. He'd found her!

Think. Think. She's watering flowers. She's not going anywhere. Right? If you water flowers you're going to stay. You're taking care of things.

He coasted by again, his car going too fast to look like a stalker and way too fast to see much. He was lucky to have that much control.

It's her! It's her!

He'd come back in the morning. Before his flight.

Should he borrow a dog?

Guy walks dog. Guy meets girl. Like on TV.

That always worked, didn't it?

He approached the two palms again and exited the complex—a bit too fast—a bit too jerky. He slowed. It didn't stop the wild shaking in his knees. Or the thrill in his chest.

Yeah, he'd make a plan—and come back in the morning.

<h1 style="text-align:center">Chapter 46</h1>

Saturday morning dawned clear and bright. Weather was great for my flight to Florida. Within a few hours I'd be in Ft. Myers. I glanced at the clock. I had time for one check through the apartment.

Appliances off: check.

Water system on outside: check.

Suitcase in the car: check.

Refrigerator: check.

All except that half loaf of bread on top.

I lifted it out of the basket and took it out front, broke it to pieces around the birdbath, and threw away the package as I returned for my purse and keys.

It hardly felt real that I was finally free to go see Grandma, and all I could think about was praying over her with the anointing oil. The first thing I would do was find it, if it wasn't with *her*, and pray over her. But didn't the Bible say to call for the elders of the church who would come and anoint? Well, maybe I could go gather a few of those too…

But at this moment, I had very little time to call Matt and make another installment in our getting-to-know-you homework. Regretfully, this whole project was turning out to be a dud. I'd never failed Peter before, and this time I was letting him *and* Grandma down.

How would I ever redeem myself?

So I dialed Matt as I drove down to the tall palms at the road to make my exit. This was probably my last chance.

One could only try.

Chapter 47

Saturday morning, Matt raced down the four-lane to the apartment complex. He rehearsed aloud the things he might say to his Sandy Beach.

The Irish setter whined quietly in the passenger seat next to him.

Matt had connected with his good buddy Zack from physics class and arranged to borrow his dog, Red. *Zack always has chicks hanging around. It has to be the dog. A girl magnet for sure.*

Matt glanced over at the Irish setter. He'd never owned a pet before, and should've asked Zack whether Red needed a seatbelt.

He shook his head. *Nah, probably not.*

Matt reached over and patted the dog's shoulder. At that moment his phone, somewhere behind Red began to ring. Whoever it was would have to wait. Matt returned his hand to the wheel as the phone continued its jingling. Right now, he was all set for a dog-walking mission. He had the plastic bags, leash, everything Red's owner said he would need for the next hour or two.

Sure hope this works.

He approached the entrance of the apartment complex with its two ancient palms. *Well, here goes nothin'.*

But as Matt passed the entrance and entered between the trees he did a double-take of the car poised to drive out. *Hey, that's the red Mustang!* Its blinker foretold a left turn. He braked and stared into his rear-view mirror.

And that has to be her at the wheel behind that phone in her hand.

His Sandy Beach. Who else would it be?

Dag nab it! He'd just missed her.

He put down the window and stuck his head out as the vehicle exited. *Yep, Florida plates.*

He slapped his hand against the wheel.

Red barked, but then whined as if to apologize for doing so. They hadn't gotten to know each other yet.

They probably never would.

He patted the dog's head. "Sorry, Red. Didn't mean to scare you."

Uncertain of what to do, Matt pulled further into the complex. He turned left toward Sandy Beach's deserted apartment.

And pulled into her parking place.

A day late and a dollar short.

He nodded and closed his eyes. *So now what?*

The dog's wet tongue dragged across his cheek and snapped him out it. No chance to mope around with old Red in the car.

He reached for the dog and pulled him close. "Thanks, pal. I needed that."

Chapter 48

Last try.

I put in my earplugs to overcome the car's noise and clicked on Matt's number. It rang and rang. A recording eventually came on and said to 'leave a message.'

There was no need to leave a message. Matt would know exactly why I was calling. And right now, I needed to keep my mind on the traffic, especially as I neared the airport.

If Matt wasn't going to cooperate, there was nothing at all I could do about it.

I pressed the hang-up button and changed lanes.

Matt backed out of Sandy Beach's parking place and headed back toward the palms at the entrance.

Time to get Red home.

He appreciated his friend's loan of the dog, but now he'd be paying for his mistake with a postponed flight. Matt had no desire to hang around town for several more hours.

But such were the breaks. At least his things were packed.

In the meantime, Red's backside was still planted on Matt's phone. He nudged the dog out of the way, retrieved it, and reminded himself to sterilize it later.

Coral, the screen said. Just as he'd suspected.

This girl was not giving up, was she?

Matt sighed and dialed her back, putting the phone on speaker. He laid it on the console as he eased into the traffic.

The dog whined and turned to Matt with a wrinkled brow. Matt had heard about dogs empathizing. Red must be unusually perceptive about his failure with Sandy Beach.

"Atta boy, Red." He patted him on the shoulder. "Girls *can* drive you crazy."

Wait. A remote conversation flashed through Matt's brain—the dog-owner's final words as Matt had driven away with Red that morning.

"If the dog whines, remember, he's not much more than a pup. Hook him up to the leash and find a grassy spot, *pronto.*"

Matt's car swerved a bit as the words sank in. Red had been patient all morning. And he'd been whining for a while. "Wait, Red, hold on, there! Just a minute, boy."

He craned his neck and scouted for a patch of grass. Not a one in sight. But campus was only a few blocks away.

Matt pressed the gas.

"Hang on, Red. Hang on."

My phone rang as I continued on my way to the airport. A peek at the screen told me it was Matt.

Well, it's about time.

However, he didn't say hello, and I could hardly make out his words. It sounded like, *Wait, Red, hold on, there! Just a minute, boy.*

Weird.

He must've pocket-dialed me. I adjusted my earplugs and tried to figure out what was going on. Car doors slammed. A dog whined. Then barked. The voice sounded like Matt again, "Good boy. That-a boy."

So Matt has a dog.

I wondered how he had time for such a thing with school. Especially *his* hard subjects.

I guess if I had time for flowers, he could care for a dog.

Eventually I shook my head and hung up.

Still your turn to call, Matt.

Within minutes, Matt dialed me back. Traffic was thickening, and the fast pace of I-26 set my nerves on edge. But I answered, thankful that I'd left the earbuds in.

Matt was laughing and blurted something out about a close call and being glad for the grass on campus.

At first, I had no idea what he was talking about.

Then I put two and two together.

Matt's pleasant manner baffled me. Besides being unlike his dad, was there some strange kind of problem with this guy, one that Grandma was protecting me from? I wondered if this getting-to-know-you activity could be her way of enlightening me without badmouthing him—her way of letting me discover his issues myself.

But that didn't make sense if she wanted us as co-successor trustees.

Arrrgh! I'd have to let this thing play out. So I offered, "That last call—when I heard your dog barking—was that a pocket dial?"

That brought out his full explanation of borrowing the dog for some *experiment* he wanted to try. He never did explain the experiment, but to hear him talk, he had me laughing too. Matt *was* a good storyteller.

So while he was in a pretty jolly mood, I spit out my next question.

"Okay, Matt, so while we're actually getting to know each other—I figure you don't believe me about having a room at your grandma's. That's okay. We can get back to that. But right now, let me ask you a few questions so I know *you're* telling *me* the truth. Fair?"

At that point the dog began to bark—an excited yelp.

"We're getting close to Zack's house," Matt said. "I'm about to drop off Red."

This could be his way of avoiding my question.

"Oh, great," Matt said. "Sit, Red. Sit!" A long pause ensued and Matt came back on. "Picture the tail of an Irish Setter beating you in the face," he said. "And the car's kind of sm….Stop it, Red. I hope I don't run into someone." The dog yelped several short bursts as if in distress. "Okay, Red. I know you love your daddy. But calm down fella. People are going to think I'm beating you."

Under the circumstances, it seemed Matt was pretty calm and had a good deal of patience.

"Get down, now. Sit. Sit. Oh, man. Red's window's half down. Hope he doesn't jump out. Hang on, Red. C'mon, now, get your head back inside. Give me a minute, Coral. I've got to park and hook his leash back on. Sorry."

Car doors slammed, more furious barking ensued, and a brief but muffled conversation told me Matt had connected with the owner.

Once again, a car door slammed, and Matt picked up the phone again. "There. Whew. Moving down the road now. What an experience."

"Sounds like you get along with dogs."

"Well, lesson learned if I can read their language," he said.

"I'm on my way to the airport," I ventured.

"I'll be down there soon. My flight lands at four o'clock." He explained the delay as some kind of *complication*.

"So Matt, can I ask you a question or two?"

"Grandma always told me her neighbor girl was away at camp. She didn't say you had a room there."

"Okay, never mind that for right now. Here's my big quiz. What is tied to the north side of the cabana railing?"

"My rope ladder, of course."

"*Your* rope ladder?" I couldn't believe my ears.

Matt could have seen pictures of the ladder. That was too easy. But that was *my* rope ladder. Grandma had it made for me. *Didn't she?*

All I could hear through Matt's phone was the traffic. For some reason, he didn't respond to my comment.

Now I was even more confused. "So Matt, tell me why you think that was your ladder."

A few seconds passed. "Well, I designed it."

"Explain, please."

Traffic was getting heavy as I neared the airport. My hands gripped the wheel as I took the exit and headed in, following the signs to correct lane. I was pretty much a granny-type driver when it came to navigating the airport, but it got easier each time I flew.

Right now, I needed to keep my wits about me as I found the long-term parking and was glad I'd given Matt an open-ended question.

I regretted not hiring a shuttle. It would've been a whole lot simpler.

Too late now. But next time… "Let me call you back, Matt. I'm busy navigating."

It didn't take very long to get my car situated, go inside, get my boarding pass, and check my bags.

Two hours seemed like a long time to sit around in an airport. But they had their reasons, I guessed. In my purse were two good novels to choose from, and I had Matt to harass.

But what I really wished I could do was call Grandma.

"She doesn't have her phone in the hospital," Peter had said. "Just call me for updates."

Well, I'll just do that, then. I dialed him up.

But Peter's phone went directly to voicemail.

And his voicemail box was full.

"Aww, Peter!" This was no time for him to desert me.

Thirty minutes later and three chapters into Frank Peretti's *This Present Darkness*, a book I'd borrowed from Grandma, I tried Peter again. Same story. Mailbox full.

I still hadn't called Matt back.

But then my phone rang. *Matt called me. Good.* The book was great, but I could use someone to talk to.

I'd hardly said hello before I blurted out, "Have you heard from Peter or Gr—*your grandma?*" I'd almost slipped up and taken possession of his grandma again. Heaven forbid. That would probably end our happy little getting-to-know-you thing. And I was beginning to enjoy Matt's company.

All but the *you-might-be-a-pathological-liar* part.

I wanted him to prove he wasn't.

"It's like Pete's dropped off the planet," Matt said. "Not since yesterday sometime. All I know is I'm on schedule."

"How soon is your flight?"

"A couple of hours from now. I need to be at the airport about noon," he said.

I couldn't imagine starting home to Ft. Myers that late. I could hardly wait to get there. "By the way, which airport are you flying out of?"

"Funny," he said. "I was going to ask you the same question."

"Well?"

"Charleston International."

My mouth dropped open. "You're kidding."

He laughed. "You think everything I say is joking or kidding or not even true."

"Look who's talking," I said. "It's you, not me. You're the one who thinks I'm not telling the truth."

"Truce, truce, truce," he said.

I could almost see a grin on his face.

"So Coral, what airport are you flying out of?"

"The very same."

"Hmmmm," he said.

I liked the tone of his voice. Manly.

"This is growing more and more interesting all the time."

"You're not off the hook, yet, though," I told him. "Tell me what are you doing right this very minute."

"I'm home now. At the apartment. Very lousy posture. One foot propped on the suitcase—arms folded, phone on my leg."

"Complete picture. Got it."

"And you?"

I chuckled. We should have done FaceTime. "I'm scooched into the corner of a chair with my coffee at my elbow and a book on my lap. Open. And it's annoying me because I need a marker." I transferred the book to the seat beside me.

"So—back to your question…" he said.

I'd almost forgotten what that was. "Go ahead…"

"Grandma's always asked me to design things for her. She wanted me to design a pirate get-away ladder for the cabana. She sent me stamps and told me to mail her the plans right away."

Very interesting. Very interesting indeed. I asked him a few more questions about where things were in the cabana. He knew everything about it. But nothing he couldn't have learned from a few photographs. He never mentioned my room.

"Okay, Matt, here comes the biggest test of all." His answer would make or break the whole story.

Inwardly, I hoped he passed it. I was enjoying our friendship, even if he was a doughy offshoot of old Sol.

"Go ahead, blast away." The smile in his voice was evident.

"Have you ever been down in the field behind Grandma's in that flowery meadow with all the grass—and goats?"

He belted out a laugh. "What are you talking about, Coral? There's no field back there. It's a stream. And tropical woods."

I sighed, not where he could hear, though, and said nothing—just let him continue. He'd passed this exam with flying colors.

"I used to go down there by the water with my matchbox cars. I'd built all kinds of forts and towns with sticks and rocks. There was no field."

He hadn't been lying.

I remembered that day like it was yesterday—the day I came back from camp and found his stuff down there. Had to be his.

"Yay! You passed," I said. "Now one more really big one."

He groaned. "Aren't you finished torturing me?

Of course, I wasn't. This would reveal even more.

"What is in the room to the back left of the cabana?"

"The—room—in the back of the *cabana*?" I could hear him puzzling over this one.

"Yes, the back left of the cabana."

"I-I'm not sure. She always told me to leave that room alone. The door was locked."

"Aha!" I hadn't realized Grandma locked it while I was gone. But I was glad. She wasn't letting some nosy old boy snoop through my things. "So you tried to peek."

He was busted, and he knew it. His laugh was contagious. I had to pull the phone away from my ear. "Well, yes, of course, I tried."

So I guess he really didn't know about it. That the room was mine.

I pointed my finger at the phone. "*That,* you ding-bat, is my *room*!"

Silence. Then, "Hmmm. I seeeeeee." I could picture him nodding. "So you *did* stay there."

A lengthy silence. This time my own. "Time for your confession, please. Admit you were wrong about me."

"I'm sorry, Coral. You weren't lying."

Matt's father would never have apologized. He'd never have put up with teasing. Rather, he'd have gone off on some other unrelated tangent.

This grandson may be created in Sol's pallid image, but as things were turning out, he was cut from a different type of cloth. A much better one.

I set the phone down and put Matt on speaker as I discarded my cold coffee, found a marker for my book, and grabbed my bag. Right now, it was time to make my way through security.

"Apology accepted," I said. "And, for your information, I *still* stay there—when I'm home."

I picked up the phone and headed for the line beginning to form at the concourse.

Somehow, knowing that Grandma locked the door of my bedroom made home seem a little more real. A little more *mine.* Even when I was absent, Grandma was looking out for me.

And my rope ladder.

She'd had Matt *design* it. A specific and intentional thing. Not a spur of the moment idea.

If one could feel the security of being wrapped in invisible loving arms, I was beginning to experience it.

Once I navigated the labyrinth of security, I found a new cozy corner and called Matt back. I hadn't really wanted our chat to end.

"I've got a question for *you*, now," he said.

Oh, boy. My turn.

"One word—why?"

Oh, dear. I knew what he meant—and the direction this might lead—and I wasn't ready to go there. Not yet. So I stalled.

"Why *what?*"

"Why did you have a room there—when you lived right next door? Why did Grandma keep this a secret?

The answer had everything to do with why she asked him to design that ladder.

"You remember when you didn't want to explain about not coming to the funeral? You'll understand if I'd rather not discuss it yet. Maybe soon. But I'm not quite there. Okay?"

"Coral, I didn't mean to pry. And if it turns out you never want to tell me, that's fine. As for my story, I'm still not quite ready either. But maybe soon, maybe soon."

I couldn't come up with a response to that, so I just sat there and pondered the situation. Was Grandma ashamed of me? Why *had* she kept me a secret? Or *him* a secret? I doubted she was ashamed. She probably thought my situation was none of his business.

If I was an embarrassment to her, she'd have ditched me long ago.

The most logical answer I could come up with was the most obvious. She had to be protecting me from something. Some flaw—in Matt?

Well, she needn't worry about me. He was a very nice guy, but I wasn't afraid of him. I was pretty sure he was harmless. Sure sounded like it when he was talking to the dog, anyway.

On the contrary. I rather liked his ways—at least over the phone.

As things stood, I'd be able to act civil when I met up with him at Peter's—and maintain that after I figured out his flaw. Liking his ways would help me look past whatever similarities he had to Sol—but those seemed to be growing fewer and fewer all the time.

If Sol had asked me that *why* question just now, he would have badgered me to death until I answered. He wouldn't have let it go. Not unless I told him straight out it was none of his business. Some people just won't quit. And Sol was the worst.

Not that I'd had conversations with him. I hadn't.

But Grandma Rosella had.

And then it struck me, Grandma didn't want me falling for Sol's offspring. She knew that a bucket of worms like that would ruin my life. And she refused to dishonor her son by badmouthing him or his offspring.

So she kept us apart. To prevent it.

Pray for my son. Pray for my son—that's pretty much all she ever said. She didn't have to tell me the rest. I'd seen it.

I loved her for that. It made her an angel in my book.

But she didn't have a thing to worry about. I was fast becoming friends with him, but I wasn't about to fall for Sol's kid.

However, I did appreciate her forewarning.

"I guess you've got your mind on your flight," Matt said. I'd almost forgotten about him hanging onto the other end of the line.

"Sorry. I guess I got lost in thought."

"I'll call you when I get to the airport," he said. "By then you ought to be in Ft. Myers."

"Yeah, Peter's picking me up," I said. "And let's call instead of texting again, okay?" I didn't want to go through that with him again. Jekyll and Hyde.

His voice was warm. "Be safe, Coral Bug."

We hung up.

Be safe? And a *nick name?*

Nope. I refused to read anything into it. I was still painfully aware of my lowly position as Grandma's *neighbor girl* who had no business in Matt's family affairs. And that was no easy rope to walk.

At least I wasn't expected to deal with Sol.

And thank goodness Matt was friendly.

It didn't matter to me at this point about Matt's appearance. He wasn't hateful. I could tolerate that.

Chapter 49

Seated on the plane I wondered about Peter's dropping out of communication with me, and if I would be able to treat him civilly now without expressing my irritation. It didn't make sense how he could just turn off his phone on me. Or not let me talk to Grandma myself.

I couldn't even ask how Grandma was. And here I was yakking on the phone and making nice conversation. It didn't seem right under the circumstances.

I had no idea what to think about anything right now, which meant it was probably best I *didn't* talk to Peter.

A worrisome mouse began to nibble on my thoughts. Peter must have a reason for not answering. Had Grandma taken a turn for the worse?

I closed my eyes and prayed that she was okay and made plans. If her purse was at the house, I would find her bottle of anointing oil and anoint her myself. I knew what the Bible said about the sick calling for the elders of the church. But this was Saturday. How was I going to do that? I'd just have to do the next best thing.

Worrying was no use. And besides, I'd read in Revelation last night that the fearful and the unbelieving would be cast into the lake of fire among other bad sinners. I'd made up my mind not to be fearful.

Whatever God had in store for me, He was in charge. And if something had happened to Grandma, if I were left alone in this world, He would be there for me once again just like He'd always been.

I would always be grateful for my miracle at age twelve when he placed her in my life.

While up in the air I made the decision to push aside all fear. Before I knew it, I had napped through my entire flight in perfect peace.

Back on the ground again, I turned on my phone. One text awaited me from Peter.

```
I'm not able to come.
Please hire an airport
taxi. Everything is okay.
```

Chapter 50

Up in the hospital room, Peter's phone dinged. It was Matt with a question or two about his grandma. For one, he couldn't remember what the name of her sickness was. Peter had already told him all that, but right now the boy was understandably distracted.

But this was no time for Peter to be texting. The doc would be working his way down this hall any time now, Peter had spotted him at the nurse's station. And he had plenty of questions for him, seeing how Rosella would be dismissed today.

He stepped away from Rosella's bedside and out into the polished hospital hallway to dial his office. He'd let the new girl field Matt's questions. She had Peter's family phone list and could text the boy from her phone.

"Just look for Matt, Sol's son, but *not Sol, mind you,*" he told her. "Remind him the sickness was called sepsis—but reassure him she's absolutely fine now. We're still up here at the hospital, but not for long. He probably won't get your text anyway, though, but we should try to answer him. He's probably already on the plane."

Back at Peter's office the new girl studied the family phone list from Peter's desk drawer. There it was, the number for Sol's son. Matt.

She pulled out her phone. He'd be confused by the strange phone number. So she'd better explain who she was in the text.

The angel grinned and covered up Matt's number with his finger. This left only Sol's number in plain view.

Time for Sol to start his little journey to the east.

The new girl pulled up her keypad and thought a minute about how she'd word the text to Matt, Sol's son.

Dear Matt, this is Cindy at Peter's office. Peter said it was called sepsis. He said you were probably on the plane by now and might not even get this. Peter's at the hospital now. Have a good flight.

She hit *send* and then packed up her purse and other items to go home.

On the way to lock up and turn out the lights, she turned and sniffed. *Hmm. Odd. Someone must have bought a new air-freshener. Roses.* She nodded. *Nice. Very nice.*

In Las Vegas, Sol stared at the words on his phone's screen and studied the number. This message was meant for Matt. That was clear enough.

And Sol's mama was dyin'.

Not without him *there. Not without old Sol.Hmph!*

"Think you're gonna pull a fast one on me?"

He tapped a quick response.

`I'm on my way. SOL`

Out in the parking lot the new girl glanced down as her phone *dinged*.

`I'm on my way. SOL`

A chill ran through her veins as she read Sol's words and realized her horrible mistake. She'd done the very thing she shouldn't have done. Peter had stressed to her *not* to tell Sol. She burst into tears.

But how? She'd been so careful. And, *oh, dear,* here she'd betrayed Peter by texting to the wrong number.

There was nothing else to do but confess to Peter. She had to. He was a courtroom lawyer, for goodness' sake, and he'd eventually get it out of her anyway.

With trembling hands, she dialed Peter, the boss that treated her so well.

No answer.

She dropped the phone on the seat and pulled out of the parking garage. A few blocks down the road, she pulled into a grocery store parking lot and tried again.

Once again, no answer.

Over and over, she tried. Finally, she had to leave Peter a voicemail and tell him the bad news. The sooner the better. Within minutes she was bawling out a recording and telling him how very sorry she was—blubbering out the truth.

Oh, dear Lord, please don't let him fire me.

Chapter 51

 y taxi-bus, just like the airport, was not crowded. Matt called me as the taxi made its way those few miles to Grandma's.

"Have you spoken with Peter lately?" I asked.

"Not a word. I can't understand this silent treatment."

"I'm trying not to worry."

"God's got this," Matt said. Up until now, I hadn't known anything about Matt's faith, and this situation was revealing another big difference between him and his dad.

"Yes, He does," I said. "I choose to believe that." I told Matt about the verse in Revelation I'd read last night, and he said he'd check it out.

"You told me you were flying out of Charleston," Matt said. "But you didn't say which school you've been attending."

"You first."

"Galena."

"Of all places." Sort of what I expected. "Me too," I said. Of all the schools in the nation and all the schools in Charleston, we'd both ended up at the same place. And we'd known nothing about each other up until now.

A long silence filled my phone as my taxi hummed over the road.

Matt finally spoke. "I refuse to doubt you this time, Coral. I'm convinced you're telling the truth. But why haven't we bumped into each other? This puzzle is just getting weirder and weirder."

No kidding. I was beginning to suspect that Grandma's influence in helping me choose a school and paying my way had been part of some grand scheme of hers. But with all the secrecy, it wasn't making much sense.

Grandma, I hope you make it through this. I've got so many questions for you.

"Back to your question…I didn't come to the funeral because Mom had just left. She just walked off."

"I'm sorry, Matt."

"When your parents aren't married," he added, "they have no strings. No obligations."

I nodded, thinking of my own messed-up family.

"And when your dad is a beast, a self-serving, narci—Sorry. When your dad is a beast, why would a woman *want* to stay?"

"I'm sorry you got caught in the middle of that, Matt. I really am."

He sighed. I could tell this was a struggle for him.

"My mother died," I told him. "And I found her. Rosella took me in." It hadn't really happened in that order, but for now it was good enough.

"I'm so sorry, Coral Bug. And I apologize for giving you a hard time."

I smiled. Waited for him to go on.

"That's just like Grandma, isn't it?" he said. "She'd never let me talk bad about Dad or Mom. *Honor your parents anyway*, she'd tell me. *And pray for them.*"

"I know," I said. "Rosella insisted on the same for my mom. She would say, *Your mama loved you, Coral, all the way to the very end. I know this. So never speak evil of her.* I can't tell you how hard it was for me to do that." As soon as the words left my mouth, I regretted saying them. Matt would think I was awful for talking bad about my mother. Especially since she'd died.

But he glossed right over it. "If it hadn't been for Grandma," Matt said, "I'd never have gone to Galena."

"We had nothing, either. Before she took me in, we were dirt poor."

"Oh, we had money, all right. Don't think that. Lots and lots. But Dad had other things to spend it on. He didn't get an education, so therefore, I didn't need one. I'm so glad Grandma stepped in."

How awful of Sol. How controlling. And greedy. I'd never met anyone like him. It was impossible for me to understand how Rosella and Eduardo had raised a character like Sol, and I'd long-since resolved within myself to never meet him. Pray for him, yes. Meet him, no.

Matt came back on. "I do understand why Grandma doesn't want my dad to know about her sickness."

"You know, I've been praying for your dad for years. Grandma—*your* grandma—asked me to do it." There, I'd slipped up and said it. I'd claimed her as my grandma.

Matt didn't seem to notice that either.

And then it hit me. I'd been worrying just now about what Matt thought of me. Why did that matter?

"It's been good getting to know you, Coral."

"So you think we're okay to go to that meeting now? We won't fuss and fight and call each other names like *Liar, liar, pants on fire?*"

Matt laughed. "Yeah, I guess we are. Absolutely!"

In the background, a loud-speaker announcement blasted through Matt's phone. "Looks like I've got to go catch that flight now," he said.

"Yes, and we're pulling up to the house now. Oh, Matt, it looks so vacant."

A sense of dread filled me as I eyed the gate's overgrown vines. I'd be entering Grandma's deserted home alone. Would it look the same as that night when they all came in and carried her away to the hospital? What would I find?

"It's going to be all right," he said, as if he could read my thoughts.

I actually hated to hang up—and wished Matt were here in person. "Thanks, Matt. I hope you have a safe flight."

"Call you soon, Coral Bug."

The taxi pulled to a stop, and I exited. My eyes fixed on Grandma's front door as I pulled open the gate, and it scraped over the seashells. I left it ajar to say *Come, come, come. I want you here. I need my people. I need my family.* Perhaps Grandma's neighbors, my uncles, would notice it and realize someone was here.

Then on second thought, I pulled the gate shut behind me.

As much as I wanted my people, truth was, I needed a little time to myself.

At that moment a text *dinged* my phone. It was Peter. *Finally.*

We're waiting for the
hospital to release your
grandma. We'll be home before you know it! Please
have your Grandpa Eduar-
do's old wheelchair handy...
not an emergency, Coral.
It's just to make things
easy. Please don't worry.

Those few words lifted a load off my shoulders. She was defi-nitely alive. Not that Peter hadn't been telling me this all along. Shells on the path crunched as I stepped past the concrete table, raking my fingers along its tiny colored tiles where my heroes still played their games. I smiled. The dust was thin, just a few days old. They'd been here.

At the deck I paused before Grandma's yellow and white awning. Its former brightness appeared so drab now above the deserted front door and lifeless windows. Without Grandma's lively personality the place was no more than a hollow space—a cave.

Stop it. She hasn't died.

I stepped up on the deck and unlocked the door.

Small trailers could build up some major heat—I expected that. But when I opened the door, the stuffiness of the room nearly sucked the wind right out of me. Grandma had always kept the place airy and fresh. I shook my head and set to work opening windows and doors. People would be coming.

I stepped toward her bedroom and paused in the doorway. *Bless them.* Somebody had taken the time to make up Grandma's bed. Probably Peter. I lifted her pillow and cuddled it against my face where I knew her halo of braids had last rested. Had they changed the pillow case too? I breathed in her scent. *Grandma.* A lump formed in my throat. I laid the pillow back down, smoothed the damp spots with my fingertips, and reached up to crank open her window. She wouldn't want me acting morbid like this.

Back at the kitchen table, I tossed out a bowl of shriveled hibiscus flowers. She had to have picked these the day she got sick, since the blooms only last a day. She'd also taken all the photos off the refrigerator and stacked them there beside her prayer list. She must have been cleaning that day too.

Well, I'd just surprise her and finish the job.

I rolled Eduardo's wheelchair away from the corner beside her living room chair and wheeled it outside in front of the gate so I could vacuum.

While I was out there, I glanced up and down the street. Still empty. I had no idea when Peter would show up with Grandma and little Yap Yap.

Back inside I ran a bucket of hot soapy water and set to work wiping down kitchen surfaces. Nothing like a fresh smell. Then I vacuumed the carpets and fluffed the cushions.

Before Grandma's illness, she'd told me she'd been working on a secret project and had a surprise waiting for me in my bedroom. Once I vacuumed the trailer, I headed out to the cabana with the vacuum cleaner.

And when I opened my bedroom door, I stopped in my tracks. *What?*

There, hanging on my dress form was the wedding gown she'd asked me to design. I flipped on the light. Pinned to the corkboard beside the light switch was the drawing I'd left that night.

She'd created this dress for me—the exact same one I had drawn.

I stepped closer. A straight chair sat immediately in front of the gown, and beside it on the floor sat Grandma's pink sewing box, along with a final, yet unattached piece of lace. She'd almost finished it.

Oh, Grandma. This is what you were doing that night, wasn't it? I bet you put off going to the doctor so you could get this done.

I took another quick trip out to the front yard and found the street still quiet. Neither Peter nor any of the heroes—who mostly took naps during this time of day—had shown up yet. But then, the gate was still shut. Obviously, no one realized I was here yet.

It was just as well, as I was enjoying this little space of time alone. So for the second time today, I left the gate shut.

I turned, brushed my fingers across the back of Eduardo's wheelchair and headed back inside to find Grandma's tote-purse. I wanted to locate her anointing oil before she got home. Of all the things that represented Grandma, that one tiny thing suited her the best and stood for what she needed most—our prayers. Not that I hadn't been praying. But anointing her with oil was especially biblical. Now if I could just put my hands on it…

I found her bag in her bedroom closet. *Thank you, Peter. For leaving everything in place.*

Her sweet purse. I hauled it into the living room and plopped down with it on the floor by the front door.

And there in the very bottom, under her wallet, I found the oil, that warm connection to everything Grandma was. I leaned against the wall and clutched it to my heart.

The minutes ticked by as I daydreamed, imagining Rosella was nearby, out in the cabana, or in her bedroom. A light breeze drifted in, ruffling the curtains and bringing with it the light twitter of birds. I breathed deep. The room was fresh now and felt more like home.

The glass vial grew warm in my hand. I rubbed my finger along its smooth side and the ridges of its lid. How many times had Rosella opened it and tipped it over on her finger—long before I ever came along. How many times had she refilled this thing over the years?

I recalled the times she'd applied the oil to my forehead or Eduardo's, those photos, and dripped it along the sidewalk around that abortion clinic to put them out of business.

Like Joshua marching around Jericho, she was a warrior in her own right. I wanted nothing more than to be just like her.

I opened the vial and dampened my finger. I drew a little oily cross on my forehead. *I set myself aside for You, Lord. Put my feet on Your path and make my ways to please You.*

I bet Rosella had said something like that at one time or another.

But just then a peripheral thought caught up with me—something I'd brushed aside while getting out the oil. I rummaged through Rosella's purse again for the brown envelope I'd seen. It felt strange digging through someone else's purse, even if it *was* Grandma's. But hadn't the envelope said *For Coral?*

There. Sure enough. I pulled it out. *For Coral*, it said on the front, in Grandma's handwriting.

"What is this?" It was unsealed.

I bent the brads and opened the flap. A gasp escaped my mouth as I slid out the stained papers. "No way."

Here was my old field trip slip with Mama's dried blood, her fingerprints, and all. I laid them across my lap.

A second stained paper, a paycheck, clung to the back of it. I peeled it off.

My fingers trembled as I pressed my knuckles against my mouth as I examined the handwriting on its backside. "Oh, my goodness," I whispered. This was a note from Mama to me, written on her last paycheck, and still attached to its stub. It must have been the only paper available as she bled out on that couch.

She must've written it the day she signed the field trip slip. Tears welled up in my eyes as I read her shaky script.

Dear Coral, I done us all wrong and I know it now. But it ain't goin to change much. I asked Jesus to forgive me like Rose once told me how. I know he done forgive me. I know. I'm sorry tho for you and your baby sister and that I ain't taken Roses advice and done things right. But old Bo, he was gonna take you, Coral. Thats why I don it. Done the abortion. Bo kept commin to the door and lookin in on you. You seen him lookin' in. Rosella knowed about it. That's why she took you in. But he knowd you was next door too. He seen you over there. He told me if I didn't do this he was gonna do bad things to you and kill you. He said he'd make sure you paid. And you wouldn't get away from him. And I know he mint bisness. I done it to prutect you. I'm sorry. But I do love you. I do. You were the best thing of my intire life. If your father could only see how good you turned out. Ask Rose about him up on the coast. You got a daddy but he's a bad mess. And he ain't much. Love, your mama

I wrapped myself around my knees and wept. Wept for not having understood. Wept for the loss of my baby sister. And wept that Rosella had protected me from the heartache of knowing.

And I wept because Mama had loved me after all.

She really had.

I finally stood. Wiped my eyes. People would be coming soon. My face probably looked like I'd been to work at a hot sauce factory.

I slid the papers back in the envelope, but kept the vial of oil.

Grandma's tote went back into the cupboard to deal with another time. I should go out to the cabana and freshen up.

So I had a father? A mess *of a father?*

For the time being, I pushed this detail into the numbest corner of my mind. Later. I'd think about it later. And it would take some time to sink in.

Whoever he was, and based on all the men my mother had dragged home, I might not want to meet him.

At least not now.

Chapter 52

Anew text from Peter dinged my phone.

```
          Be there in thirty minutes.
          Never mind about the wheel-
          chair. She doesn't need it.
          Uncles all coming in thirty
          minutes with food.
```

I rolled my suitcase out to my room and opened it on the bed. It took me a few minutes to sort through my things and freshen up. But I was glad I did. I slipped on a fresh sundress, one of Grandma's favorites, a yellow and white print. I added a thin string of pearls and matching wedge heels. My hands shook as I fixed a matching flower in my hair just for Grandma.

For now, there was so much going on I was beginning to feel a little overwhelmed. But then, I stopped myself in mid-worry. It's Grandma that should be overwhelmed. I needed to be strong for her.

I shut my door and headed back the kitchen where I'd set the photos in a shallow box while I cleaned. I had every intention of going through them as I waited on the company to arrive.

The way Grandma liked to pray over everyone—it disappointed me that she'd never put up a single picture of her grandson. Leaving him out seemed so out-of-character for her. I'd even reminded her—numerous times. And could never squeeze a straight answer out of her as to why she hadn't.

Grandma, always full of mystery.

Guests were on the way. I should hurry up.

I'd raced around, tossed tablecloths over the mosaic table and a card table I set up on the deck. I'd brought out TV tables and folding chairs, set out some napkins, fresh hibiscus flowers, and lined up the plastic utensils and plates by the time my phone rang. I glanced at the screen. *Peter. Finally.* He was sitting in his car in front of the hospital, waiting on the nurse to wheel Grandma downstairs. It wouldn't take them ten minutes after that. "She's in great shape," he said. "She can't wait to see you two."

Matt still hadn't arrived. I hadn't heard a peep out of him.

"There is this one thing—and I know this might not be the best timing," I said, and told Peter about the brown envelope. "It's Mama's letter. I have a dad."

"Um hmm." Peter's response told me he already knew about it.

"This is so much all at once, Peter," I said. "I'm feeling a little fritzed-out, you know?"

"I can see how this letter would upset you. Look. Don't you worry about it for now. I can help if you want. Or if you don't feel like doing anything about it at all, it's A-OK." His voice was friendly, reassuring, and took a load off my shoulders. "For the time being, let's concentrate on your grandma and her big homecoming."

"Thank you, Peter."

If Peter had been there with me, I'd have given him a big old hug.

Chapter 53

I was looking forward to meeting my new friend, Matt. And even if his outward appearance revealed he was a clone of his pale, unattractive, money-hungry, narcissist father, on the inside I knew he was nothing like the old guy. I guessed that maybe Rosella in all her wisdom was trying to keep me from stereotyping him, despite his resemblance to Sol—a thing she knew I would struggle with. She'd been telling me that looks aren't everything, and surely that worked in the negative direction as well as the positive. She was so very wise, and I was beginning to catch on.

If only I turned out half as wise as Rosella, I'd be happy.

Maybe that's why she was so adamant about us getting acquainted before we got together with Peter at his office. She needn't worry. I'd figured out that Matt had his Grandfather Eduardo's genes. And maybe even his brave heart.

Those good attributes had skipped right over a generation and landed on Matt. But how, I did not know.

For a split second I lifted the kitchen curtain and peeked out of the front window. A good-size group was already gathering. I focused on no one in particular but observed familiar bald heads, dear smiling faces, white shirts and ties, and a cloud of cigar smoke around the front table. With everyone dressed up so nice I could only imagine the wonderful after-shaves and colognes. I couldn't wait to get out there with them.

And to think, I'd never even opened that gate. I guess Peter had called them.

As always, it satisfied me to know how completely surrounded I was by such amazing acceptance. I twisted the front door knob and sneaked out, not wanting to draw attention to my late entry.

Those on the deck greeted me in friendly fashion, and like the gentlemen our friends and heroes were, several rose to their feet. "Oh, my goodness, thank you, sit down. It's okay," I said, giving them hugs and continuing to circulate and greet everyone. These men were old. They didn't need to stand up for me, something they'd started doing for me after high school.

I grinned and stepped along the seashell path toward the table. I leaned in to embrace one more of them.

But as I glanced across his shoulder near the fence, the figure seated in the wheelchair with Yap Yap in his arms took my breath away. I gasped. My knees weakened and I nearly collapsed—not because of my wedge heels, either.

For a split second I thought I was seeing things.

There, with his back to me, in rapt conversation with tio Ignacio, sat a handsome young silhouette, the spitting image of my grandpa, but with dark hair instead of gray—the same size, same coloring—

Of course, it wasn't Eduardo. People don't come back to life like that. But oh my, this man was carved from the same block of wood. Who was he?

Tio Ignacio, seated on the concrete bench near the wheelchair, looked across the young man's shoulder toward me. "Well, well," he said, "look who the angels brought back to town. Coral, *mija* so good to see you." He rose and came around to hug me. Yap Yap had now leaped down and circled my feet. He bounced on his hind legs for attention. I leaned down to give him a quick pat.

I straightened and opened my arms for tio Ignacio. "Oh, tio," I said, "It's so good to see you."

We traded big hugs as the young man twisted around in his wheelchair and stood.

And I'm sure I gaped like an idiot.

Because when he turned, I found myself gazing up into the face of a very handsome, but much younger cut-out of Eduardo—all six feet something of him.

Matt twisted in his seat as Uncle Ignacio set the dog down in response to the female voice behind him and stepped around his chair.

"Coral, so good to see you, *mija*," Ignacio said.

Coral? Matt stood. He'd finally get to meet the neighbor girl.

But as Matt turned, his breath caught.

For there, gazing straight at him, with her arms around Ignacio, stood his Sandy Beach.

Flower in her hair and all.

Chapter 54

Across the street in the front seat of Peter's shiny vehicle, Grandma nudged Peter's shoulder. "Look at that crowd."

Peter's deeply tinted windows had kept the crowd from noticing them. "Yep," he grinned. Then he reached in his coat for his phone. "I've got a little voicemail I want you to listen to. It's the new girl at the office."

"What does that have to do with anything?" Rosella said.

Peter punched some buttons and played the new girl's voicemail about Sol being on his way. He grinned.

Grandma crossed her arms and chuckled. "So he thinks I'm dying. We'll see about that."

Peter shrugged. "He had to learn about your hospital visit some time or other."

Grandma swatted his arm. "Don't you fire that little girl, either."

"Wasn't planning on it. But this is gonna be some kinda show when Sol comes to town." He put the phone back in his jacket. "How are you feeling? Are you ready to go on in there and greet everyone?"

"As long as I've got a chair, and we stay outside under the mango trees. That's all I need. I'm tired of being cooped up."

But before Peter opened the car door, Grandma laid her hand on his arm. She pointed toward Matt and Coral. "Look. They're talking. See! I knew it. All they had to do was meet."

Peter followed her eye and chuckled aloud. "Right again, as always, *abuelita.*"

He moved to open the door, and she stopped him. "Wait. Don't open the door yet. Let's see what happens."

He raised an eyebrow as they watched. "Just think, now we have Coral's daddy to look forward to."

"You found him? He's alive?" Grandma said.

"Up along the Forgotten Coast somewhere. Has a little hole-in-the-wall restaurant by the docks."

"Forgotten Coast? I've never heard of that."

"Up around the big bend of Florida. It's the Gulf Coast. All we've got to do is look him up."

"Oh, dear. You make it sound so simple. *All we've got to do is look him up*, huh? That makes me a little nervous."

He turned back to the window. "That makes two of us. But there's no hurry. I shouldn't have even mentioned it yet."

"I'll be ready for a trip…just give me a little time to rest up. I don't want her up there by herself."

"I hear you," Peter said. "I'll be right there with you. Who knows? We might even get up there before old Sol gets here—since he doesn't fly."

Grandma swatted Peter's arm and laughed. "Wouldn't that be a good one? Him thinking I'm dying and me off on a vacation. Makes me want to leave today."

Peter held up one finger. "*If* Coral wants to see her dad."

Grandma nodded, more sober now. "Yes, *if* she wants to. I'm not forcing her into anything."

"She at least deserves the choice."

They eyed each other and nodded together.

Chapter 55

As Ignacio and I traded hugs the handsome young man's eyes held mine. It seemed as if he wanted to speak, but then he stopped. He tipped his head in greeting.

I'd seen this man before—beside Galena's outdoor vending machines. He and that guy in the wheelchair—standing there waving at me. And that smile. I'd never forget that.

But this did not make sense. Rosella and Eduardo had no relatives—other than Matt. So who was this handsome guy? I quickly scanned the crowd, the men at the table, the ones on the deck. Where was Sol's doughy fair-skinned son?

Wait. Wait. Wait. No way. This can't be Matt—the guy I've been talking on and off with all day.

Oh, dear. I'd almost lost my manners. I stepped forward, extended my hand only to find it trembling worse than my legs. "Would you be the mysterious Matt?"

He grinned.

Tio Ignacio introduced us, but I hardly heard him. My awareness of the crowd faded along with the hum of their voices, and I was dimly aware but thankful that tio Ignacio had quickly gathered up Yap Yap and carried him away into the crowd. I struggled to piece it all together.

If this was Sol's son, he looked nothing like his dad.

"You're sure you're Matt?"

What a stupid comment. But I'm not too witty at times like this.

He laughed that familiar laugh I'd grown to like over the phone and gripped my hand in both of his. I guess he *was* Matt, then.

He smiled at me with those melty-brown eyes, a prince with deep dimples. He nodded. "So you're Coral."

I grinned back, stupefied and mute, and afraid my eyes were going to roll up in my head, and I'd fall backwards into the seashells.

Out of my mouth spilled another dumb thing. "It's so nice to finally put a face to the name."

And now, as I stood there it all began to make sense. *Oh, Rosella.* All my comments about Eduardo's good looks… No wonder she refused to display her grandson's picture. Not if he looked like *this*.

Before I could get my thoughts on straight, though, voices around me were speaking out, "Look. It's Rosella. She's here!"

I turned and searched the street for her.

Grandma! She stood there by what must have been Peter's new car and clung to his arm. Somehow I'd missed him driving up.

I turned to push the wheelchair out the gate. But Matt leaned in. "Allow me?" He reached for the chair-handles while sending me a wink at the same time.

I know I turned red. But I trotted along behind him. That man could move.

"Excuse us," he said, "We must take the throne to the queen."

The uncles around me chuckled.

Out in the middle of the street, Peter held up a hand for the eager crowd to stay put as he and Matt helped Grandma get situated in the wheelchair. She didn't seem to need it, but she'd lost a few pounds, and considering her pale complexion I realized having the chair handy was a good thing.

It was all I could do to wait those few seconds, and then, "Grandma!" I dove in between them and hugged her sweet neck.

"Coral, honey," she whispered against my shoulder. "So good to see you."

I couldn't help but sob a little, but I did what I could to hold back. She wasn't dead, after all. She was alive and well.

I didn't want to let go, but I finally stood.

Then Matt latched onto her. "I'm so glad you're better. We love you so much, and we've missed you so much." When he let go he wiped his eyes.

Peter started to take the chair's handles and turn the chair around to go in the gate, but I stopped him. "Wait. Please. I've been waiting all week for this one thing." I opened the anointing oil I'd been clinging to for the last half hour. "I'm sorry I didn't have time to find any elders from the church. But let me, please."

She knew exactly what I meant. And I'm glad the crowd had some patience. I only needed a few seconds.

I dabbed my finger with oil and drew a cross on her forehead. I leaned close. "Lord, thank you so much," my voice broke at those words, but I kept going. "Thank you for bringing my grandma back. Thank you for helping her. Now, please strengthen her and give her back the good health that she had before. I ask in Jesus' name."

We all said *Amen* together, and moved across the street with Grandma gripping Matt's hand on one side, and mine on the other. She pressed mine to her wet cheek and gave it a kiss.

Beyond the gate the crowd swallowed her up with their loving words and embraces.

Matt lagged back behind the chair and tried to digest what he had just witnessed in Coral.

He'd never met a girl so much like his Grandma.

<h1 style="text-align:center">Chapter 56</h1>

W-wait just a minute," I said, closing gate behind us. My mission with the oil was accomplished, and my thoughts had settled at finally seeing her.

With everyone focused on Grandma now and the hearty platters upon the tables, Matt and I caught ourselves eyeing each other. We hadn't finished our introductions. "I've got to figure something out," I said. "Could you come over here to the steps for a minute?"

I needed to sit down anyway, to get the shakes out of my legs and to keep from fainting.

"But first let me run inside and get something."

How odd—ducking inside like that suddenly reminded me of that first night when Rosella popped back inside the trailer and came back out with the cookies and the Afghan for me. It seemed so long ago.

I found the box of photos on the kitchen table and came back out. And there, Matt and I settled side by side on the steps, with me trying not to tremble to pieces, and him smiling with those dimples. His eyes never left mine. That, by itself, unnerved me. Made me shiver.

I opened my hand with the vial of anointing oil still in it. "I guess you could say I found this." Matt and I had talked about the oil before. I clutched it to my cheek and smiled. "I'm so glad I finally got to pray for her."

A spark flickered in his eyes. But he said nothing. Just grinned some more.

"Let me show you something else, though," I said, digging through the box of photos.

"Is that roses you're wearing?" he asked.

I touched the flower in my hair.

"No, no," he said. "Not that, I'm talking about a perfume."

I smelled it now, too. "Wait. Maybe it's this." I took the lid off the anointing oil and sniffed. Nothing. I sniffed the box. Nothing. I shrugged. "This happens now and then," I told him, replacing the lid. "But look around. No roses. I'm not sure why it happens."

He just grinned as I continued my search through the photos.

I found the two I was looking for. "Okay, this is Eduardo," I said, holding up the first photo, his elderly likeness. No doubt about that. Then I pulled out the other photo, the younger version of Eduardo. "But this one…" I turned it over for the first time ever, and glanced at the back—and my mouth dropped open. My face probably turned ten shades of red.

The answer had been there all along. I clamped my fingers across my mouth.

At that point I didn't need to ask Matt a thing. It all made sense.

"Oh, how silly of me," I said. There on the back in a twelve-year-old's handwriting were the words that had been there through all those years—To Grandma with love, Matt. And there was that same peculiar lower-case e as on my gardening system directions. I flipped it over again. "This is *you*, then."

I let out an exasperated sigh. "You won't believe this, but all this time I thought Grandma had two pictures of Eduardo. And she never straightened me out. There you were on her refrigerator the whole time—year after year—right in front of my eyes. I am so embarrassed. You wouldn't believe the hard time I gave her about not putting up her grandson's picture."

With a smile he took the pictures from me and placed them with the vial of oil in the box. "Grandma has her ways, doesn't she?"

It was a good thing Grandma had kept such a tight rein on me. I'd have fallen in love with his picture—based solely on his good looks.

Her words still echoed in my ears. *Oh, honey, that's nice, but relationship is more than just looks. It's about friendship and character first. Looks aren't bad, but good looks, honey, by themselves? They will trip. You. Up. Please, I never want you to fall for somebody's looks.*

Grandma wanted it genuine. So in her own way she kept me out of that trap.

I held my breath as her words about not adopting me returned. "How would you like to be dear Sol's sister? Just think, that would make you my grandson's *aunt.*"

I gasped and realized how strange that would have been. *Thank you, Jesus, that I am not Matt's aunt. Thank you, thank you, thank you.*

Had Grandma imagined this moment way back then? Devised some grand plan?

I doubted it. She wasn't manipulative.

What about when she insisted that I design that wedding gown—and then turned right around and made it for me?

One day I'd have to put all these puzzle pieces together.

Then there was that design for the grandmother-of-the-bride dress. Of all things. At Grandma's request. That one was still waiting to be created next semester in Charleston.

Truthfully, I had begun to suspect she'd planned it for her funeral.

Grandma always kept a pocketful of secrets.

What didn't make sense, though, was that except for the scholarships, and co-successor trusteeships, she'd never overtly tried to manipulate my love life. General advice, yes. But nothing more. *Nope, nope, nope. That's all that was, just a bunch of interesting coincidences.*

Grandma did pray a lot, though. So maybe keeping her mouth shut was simply her way of trusting God.

Oh, I would never understand! It exhausted me to even wonder about it. I had so many questions.

Matt's voice interrupted my thoughts. "You know what Grandma says about that, don't you—those smells like roses—or jasmine, or something nice like that?"

"Oh? She's never mentioned it."

"It could be an angel nearby."

"An angel? Like—guardian?"

"That's what she told me."

I set the box on the steps wrapped my arms around my knees. Princely looks or not, I had no doubt Matt had turned into a nice friend, and perhaps even a man after my own heart. Obviously, he was interested in things I valued.

Matt stood. "Are you hungry?"

"Starving," I said, and ducked inside to drop off the photo box.

When I returned Matt did something I never expected. He opened his hand and whispered, "May I?" And then he took mine in his as we joined the celebration.

Acknowledgements

I want to thank all my wonderful Beta readers, Mickey and Linda Cruey, Cynthia McFarland, Sonja and Abi Lonadier, and my Word Weavers—Marian Rizzo, Dianne Kitts, Elsie Bowman, Doris Hoover, Karen Skirpan, Pam O'Brien, Devonna Alison, Robin Collison, Yeny Rowley, Leah Taylor, Delores Kight, and Sue Montgomery. Thank you for all your critiques and worthy advice. Thank you, Ivette Mateo, for your expert wisdom on Co-executorships. Thank you, fellow Joy of Writing members, and bless you Sonja and Abi Lonadier, you are always there for me. Faithful Fay Lamb, my editor, you are always straight with me. You scold (ever go kindly) when it's earned and help me iron it all out. You are a godsend. What I've learned from you can never be measured. Dear Chuck and Delores Kight, you are mighty cheerleaders, always. I love you. Fay Mercer, thank you for astute insight, and good ideas. Mike Parker, my publisher, a wise man after God's heart, I am eternally grateful, and to Jenny Eggers of Jenny E Photography, my gratitude for both of you will never fail. And of course, to my dear husband Danny for his encouragement and suggestions, and Gabrielle, my unfailing best cheerleader of all times. Thank you all.

About the Author

Jennifer Odom is a 5th generation Floridian. Her love of the land and its rich history reach back to the 1860s when her great great grandfather migrated to his new homestead in Central Florida near the railroad. Orange groves and farming busied the family while one child and her spouse established the general store and served as station-master for the thriving depot. Reflecting this love of Florida and its people, Jennifer has written human interest stories for the *Ocala Star Banner* and gardening articles for the *Ocala Gazette*. Her fiction is published in *Splickety* and *Clubhouse Jr.* magazines, as well as *Maine Review's Juxtaposition*. Her fourth novel, *Under the Mango Trees* is set in Fort Myers, Florida, and is the first in her heart-warming *Coral Series*. Her *Black Series* (suspense/mystery) includes *Summer by the Black Suwannee, Stranger with a Black Case*, and *Girl with a Black Soul*.

Jennifer is a multi-award winning veteran teacher and writer, selected as Teacher of the Year at her Florida Blue Ribbon School, and Writer of the Year at the Florida Christian Writers Conference. Connect with Jennifer online at:

jenniferodom.com

And now, a sneak peek at:

Along the Forgotten Coast
Book 2 of The Coral Series

C oral, weren't you listening?" From behind the steering wheel Peter Cordero glanced my way. The mirrored sunglasses hid his expression, but it was clear to me he was enjoying this ride up the coast in his brand-new car.

However, his endless courtroom stories were getting to be pure torture right now. I nodded and smiled from the passenger seat, anyway. After all, he was doing this for me.

My response satisfied him, and he jumped right back into his stories. Meanwhile, for the millionth time I checked the passenger-door mirror for the black Mustang where Matt and my not-really-flesh-and-blood Grandma followed behind us.

I loved her as if she were, though.

What I really wanted was to trade places with Grandma back there so I could squeeze in some conversation with Matt Flores, that very handsome grandson of hers. I'd grown to like him a lot over the past few days.

The four of us had now made good progress north on Highway 27 toward Carrabelle, Florida. But so far I was stuck in the front vehicle with Peter and his stories.

I could tell Matt wanted to get a word in with me, too.

On the way out of our last coffee stop Matt had sauntered over to me beside Peter's car and flashed that gorgeous smile of his.

"Hi, Coral, I've been hoping we'd get a word in edge-wise, but…"

Then, before he could finish his sentence, Peter stepped over to us in that uber-polite way of his, which always lets him get away with doing the stinkiest things. "Could you excuse us please for just one minute, Coral?" Then with his arm around Matt's shoulder, he took him off to the side. "Say, listen, I was just thinking…" I hardly heard the rest, but it was some detail regarding that co-executorship meeting back in Ft. Myers.

While they talked, I knelt down beside Grandma and visited with her a little, a very pleasant interlude. Having been very ill lately, she seemed to be holding up fairly well so far. But Peter kept Matt cornered and talking for at least five minutes.

The nerve!

Then it was time to go.

Forget about my previous conversation with Matt. Peter was done. He ushered Matt back to the Mustang, punched the air with Latino enthusiasm, and said, "Come on, everyone, let's keep on driving and get as far as we can before Grandma gets tired." Then he added, "Grandma Rosella, are you still comfy back there with Matt?"

Grandma grinned. And was that a wink? "Oh, Matt's a great driver. Very comfortable."

Guess this was planned.

Time to climb in. Matt traded me a grin for my wave, and then we headed out.

I think Peter was enjoying the torture. I really do.

Is this the way father-figures acted?

Peter had always stood in like that for me, full of advice. And he'd always been there when I needed him.

But this!

Ever since we left Ft. Myers, Peter had plied me with advice. More than usual, it seemed. And between calls from his office, he offered odds and ends of wise counsel like don't rush a relationship. Afterwards, he insisted I catch him up on everything about school up in South Carolina.

Since when had Peter wanted to know all these details about my sewing designs?

And now he had moved on to telling stories about the courtroom.

Guessing by his enthusiasm and occasional grins into the

rear-view mirror, he knew exactly how aggravating he was being. And he was driving me crazy.

Since that last Burger King coffee/restroom stop in Chiefland, I'd gotten comfy with a pillow, tuned him out, and had almost fallen asleep as he fielded a few more phone calls.

"Coral, were you listening to that last call?"

I stirred. "Sorry, drifted off, Peter."

"That was the home health nurse's agency. She'll be coming by every few days to check on Grandma. Up in Carrabelle."

I fluffed my pillow. "We'll take good care of her, Peter."

"Food. Good food, now. Plenty of rest. Don't let her exert herself."

I knew Grandma's recovery from sepsis would be a long and hard journey. "She'll be in good hands with Matt and me," I mumbled.

He turned and smiled. "I know that. But I had to say it anyway."

Eventually we slowed. I sat up. Our little caravan had now turned west around the Bend of Florida. Oh, dear. It wouldn't be long now. I'd get to see my father, my real father I'd only recently learned existed from papers my mother left before she died. But I wasn't at all sure about meeting him. Based on my mother's past history of men, he could very likely be just another pedophile or criminal.

But Peter had located him. My only living relative.

I could have put this trip off a long, long time, this going up the coast to meet him.

But here we were checking the man out. At Grandma's insistence.

Oh, Matt and I had tried to postpone it. To let Grandma get well first.

"I almost missed it entirely," she said. We all knew she'd almost died. "So no, dear. Wild horses can't keep me away. Besides, you all know Sol is on the way."

Sol! That old money-hungry creature thought his mother was dying. Then, to add to the confusion, Sol was Matt's dad. So far, though, he didn't seem to be like his father at all.

But Grandma wanted to turn the tables on Sol by clearing out of town.

"It's a free country," Peter had said. "We can't stop her."

I hoped for Sol's sake it didn't backfire. She'd better not end up in the hospital again because of him.

"Listen, now, Coral," Peter said, interrupting my thoughts. His voice took on a serious tone. "Here's what I've really needed to say to you this whole time.

"If you even get a hint you want out of this place, just call me. I'll be there. We'll toss your stuff in the car, and head right on back down to Fort Myers. No questions asked. You're under no obligation to stay, or meet, speak to, or accept this person as family. He's never been in your life, and he doesn't have to be now. He doesn't even have to know you're in town. Remember, I'm here for you."

"I appreciate that, Peter. I really do."

I studied the man's face as he turned his attention back to the road.

Could any real-live father be any more thoughtful, caring, or protective? I doubted it.

Yes, there was always Peter.

Ralph stepped into the darkness and fog and snapped the cottage door firmly shut behind himself. Not quite a slam, but a clear rebuff to Millie's obvious hints inside. He didn't need no dang wife. He slung his work apron over his shoulder, the one she'd laid out all clean and pressed by the door just now, and swiped his knuckles across his mouth, scraping away the bacon grease. Nah, he didn't give a clamshell how wifely she wanted to act. It made no never-mind to him that she got up every morning at four—to cook him bacon, eggs, and toast. Ralph wasn't falling for any of her tricks. Sure, that was all nice. She was nice too. But he didn't need no wife. Didn't need to be tied down.

Didn't need no kids.

That's the way things were, and that's the way they'd stay.

He stalked along the broken sidewalk for several blocks, but thoughts began to nibble around his brain as a picture of Millie's big brown eyes filled his mind. His pace diminished. Millie did mean well. He should have at least kissed her goodbye. No need to hurt her feelin's. Maybe he should turn around… Enh. He was already late. He'd make it up to her in a few hours when she came in to work. Ralph turned into the next street. Within a block he reached the side porch of Aunt Allie's ancient corner store. The overhanging mulberry limbs nearly hid her stop sign. At this hour she was asleep inside. Still, he stepped quietly.

Aunt Allie, not his real aunt, but dear to him nonetheless, he'd studiously dodged for the last twenty years.

Paused at the sign, like he did every morning, Ralph studied the sounds from across the highway. Sounds of the ocean. Well…the Carrabelle River. Same thing. It was all connected.

He cocked his head to concentrate on the sounds and smells around him. And this morning not a frond rustled. Not a wave slapped. No hint of a storm today. He breathed in the usual heavy odor of low tide—decaying oysters and marsh mud, and tipped his ear toward the faint racket of fishermen up the river at the icehouse. Sounds filtered easily across the water. The voices, one of them surely his old friend Zeke's, mixed together with the clatter and bang of ice loading into their refrigerator-sized chests for today's catch.

Ralph leaned over, picked up a stone, and rolled it between his fingers. He zeroed in on the carved Captain's Table sign two blocks away. The sign Ralph carved as a gift when Dad bought the building.

Before Ralph's rotten decisions.

If only he could go back. Carry out his and Zeke's childhood plans—to endure the rigor of boat life, ride the waves of an angry black sea, or squint into the blinding ripples of a watery sunrise. But then, Zeke…

Why Ralph kept him at arm's length he couldn't say—but then— yes he could. And the reason was lame.

Zeke could pry the truth out of anyone. Even Ralph.

So Ralph stayed away.

He inhaled and hurled the stone. And just like most every other morning his rock missed the sign and disappeared into the darkness. He shook his head and moved on down the incline.

Out in Las Vegas, Sol burst out of his office. "My mother's dyin', let me borrow your car, Eddie."

"But…"

"You don't expect me to drive my new Mercedes all the way to Florida, do you? I haven't even got the new worn off."

Eddie stared at the register.

"My mother's dyin', Eddie."

"But…"

"Look." Sol held up his key ring. "See these keys? You get to drive my car. Home to work. Work to home. That's all you drive, anyway, right?"

Sol was quite aware Eddie only lived a few blocks away at his mother's place. Most all high school kids lived at home with their mothers. School was out and Eddie wasn't done with school.

Eddie stared through the plate glass windows to the silver Mercedes parked front and center out on the street. He turned his eyes to Sol. "Me? Drive that?"

"Heck yeah."

Eddie's brows rose and his head tilted as if to say, I guess so.

"The keys are back in my office. You open and close the shop every day like I've shown you." Eddie was dependable. Good to lean on when Sol didn't feel like opening or closing. "You've been wantin' more hours, right?"

"I'm…I'm not sure about my car, though. How it runs."

"Oh, it'll do."

Anything that shiny ought to run just fine.

Back in the office Sol, removed the Mercedes key from the office key ring and dropped it in his pocket. Eddie could walk back and forth to work. Wasn't that far, really. And Sol would just say, *whoops, sorry, I forgot.*

Ralph had taken no more than a half-dozen steps between the fog-slippery lines of Highway 98 before lights approached from behind, thrusting his shadow post-haste in the opposite direction. Ralph scrambled over to the limestone parking lot in front of Aunt Allie's store. A massive produce truck thundered by, well above the speed limit. Ralph lifted his arm in a universal salute and yelled a curse-word. He'd love to be a cop right now.

Seconds later the vehicle swung in hard behind the Captain's Table. His restaurant.

Oh, wait. Today was produce day.

He took off sprinting.

After four years in the Army, Ralph still tried to keep in shape. Even after sixteen years. Like today, most of the time he walked to and from work. He watched his weight, and even jogged a little. Still, he craved more activity. Manly things. Not the activity of standing in a restaurant, but real activity.

Breaths came quick and his arms pumped as he neared the corner of his three-story building in time to meet the produce man. His lungs were barely stressed—and he was proud of it. No sir, he'd never let himself go.

But around back he pulled up short. There stood the scraggly silhouette of Larry, his pimple-faced cook—all lit up by the truck's red brake lights. Their brilliance dimmed as the driver climbed out of his truck and headed around to open it up. Ralph gazed at Larry's shadowy form. Well, well, well. For once the kid was on time. But there he stood smoking a dang cigarette. Oblivious to Ralph. Messing up the air. Ralph hated cigarettes at his back door and didn't want the smoke drifting into his kitchen.

Mew! One of the restaurant's kittens—Ralph's orphaned kittens—no bigger than a sandpiper—mewed by Larry's foot. The boy lowered his cigarette.

Ralph opened his mouth.

But by then Larry had already scooped up the little furball with his foot and sailed it into the palmettos behind the truck. "Get away from me you rodent!"

The cat landed safely, but still….

The driver, with his back turned, missed the whole ugly scene. But now he turned, made eye contact with Ralph and paused, probably recognizing him as the guy he'd almost plowed down just now.

Larry caught the driver's gaze and twisted around, aware now, too, of Ralph's presence. He froze. Stood there with a blank expression.

Ralph's fists curled.

Yeah. Everybody knew how Ralph felt about those cats.

What Ralph did next might have been a little different had the produce man not been standing right there.

Ralph signaled for Larry to come forward and pivoted as the kid approached, keeping his back to the produce man.

Ralph gritted his teeth. "You got two choices, punk. You kitten-kicker. Bully."

The kid glanced at Ralph's tattooed biceps and swallowed hard as a second kitten moved into the space between them. Mew!

Ralph pointed toward the bushes. Took a step toward Larry. "I could send you sailin' into the bushes like that…."

Larry blinked, stepped back, but his eyes remained steadfast on Ralph's unflinching glare.

"Or you can take off runnin' back home to your mama." Ralph spat the last word. He leaned into the kid's face and the next two words came out nice and slow. "Now choose!"

The boy nearly fell into the gravel as he spun around, and took off running down the road where Ralph had just come from. He didn't live far, of course.

"And don't come back," Ralph yelled. "Oh. And just for your information," he added, "cats ain't rodents."

He turned to find the delivery boy gaping in his direction, his truck still unopened. "Stupid kid," Ralph said. "Nobody kicks my kitties around."

Also Available From

Wordcrafts Press

Land that I Love
by Gail Kittleson

Paint Me Fearless
by Hallie Lee

Little Reminders of Who I Am
by Jeff S. Bray

Oh, to Grace
by Abby Rosser

Maggie's Song
by Marcia Ware-Wilder

You've Got It, Baby!
Mike Carmichael

www.WordCrafts.net

www.ingramcontent.com/pod-product-compliance
Lightning Source LLC
Chambersburg PA
CBHW031010190726
48286CB00003BA/778